TINA INTO TWO
WON"T GO

TINA INTO TWO WON'T GO

BY ELFIE DONNELLY

translated from the German by
ANTHEA BELL

FOUR WINDS PRESS
New York

Originally published in German as *Tina durch Zwei geht nicht*.
Copyright © 1982 by Cecilie Dressler Verlag, Hamburg.
English translation copyright © 1983 by Andersen Press Limited.
First American edition 1983 by Four Winds Press.
Originally published in the English language in 1983 by
Andersen Press Limited in association with Hutchinson Limited,
19–21 Conway Street, London W1P 6BS.
Manufactured in the United States of America

10 9 8 7 6 5 4 3 2 1

The text of this book is set in 12 pt. Fournier.

Library of Congress Cataloging in Publication Data
Donnelly, Elfie.
Tina into two won't go.
Translation of *Tina durch zwei geht nicht*.
Summary: After her parents' recent divorce, eleven-year-old Tina
and her family are unable to come to terms with the changes in their
lives until Tina's father kidnaps Tina at Christmastime.
[1. Divorce—Fiction] I. Title.
PZ7.D7193Ti   1983   [Fic]   83-5563
ISBN 0-590-07912-3

TINA INTO TWO WON'T GO

FOREWORD

The foreword begins with an introduction to the characters in this story. They include:

TINA Fechner: Tina is eleven years old, brown-haired, not exactly skinny, moderately good at schoolwork, likes playing with words, loves the water so much that she would like to be a fish.

TIM Fechner: Tim is seven, is brown-haired and not exactly skinny, just like his sister. He can eat six pancakes in four minutes flat, still likes going to school, and loves Tina.

ANGELICA Fechner: Tim and Tina's mother, has always been a bookworm, which is why she became a librarian. Normally she is a very cheerful person, doesn't feel quite grown-up, doesn't want to be quite grown-up, either. Hates cooking but cooks well.

KARL Fechner: Tim and Tina's father, doesn't like football, loves cooking but cooks badly. Not very tall, not very fat; very handsome indeed. Has a mustache. Is inclined to be sad and gets plenty of opportunities for that in the story.

CACTUS Fechner: not a plant, but a dog with a sort of piebald coat. Lives mainly on carpet fringes, but will happily eat other things, too. Often worries, but nobody knows about that.

SLOW-AND-SOLID Fechner: the quietest member of the family. Very pleasant company, although she doesn't always come out of her shell: Slow-and-Solid is a tortoise. Everyone likes her.

And now for the rest of the foreword.

None of the Fechners could have said what was really the beginning of the end. A few small stones rolled away and set a whole avalanche going. Karl and Angelica Fechner had been married for twelve years. They liked each other and were happy with the little house they rented not far from the city; with their children; with the dog, Cactus, and the tortoise, Slow-and-Solid; and with what money they had. As an insurance agent, Karl could make his own schedule. If he sold a lot of insurance policies he made a lot of money; if he was lazy or had bad luck he earned less.

They never had serious financial worries, because Angelica was in charge of the Children's Library. Tim and Tina used to go and sit in the library in the afternoon and do their homework. On Sundays the family went on trips together. Everything seemed to be all right, until . . .

The first thing Tina noticed was that Mother and Father had stopped kissing each other good-bye. It was almost as if neither of them noticed it themselves. Mother stopped asking Father about his work. Father did not seem to mind what sort of day Mother had had. Mother began cleaning up after Father. If he put a newspaper down on the table Mother would put it—very pointedly—in the special basket she kept for newspapers. And Father began complaining if breakfast wasn't ready on time. Before, he always made breakfast himself.

Those were the first little stones rolling away. Tina sometimes felt as if the house were shrinking, because she kept avoiding her parents and realized that she felt happier at friends' houses than at her own. Tim began acting like a baby again and wet his bed. At first, this was the only sign that Tim, too, was aware of the changes in the Fechner household.

Mother went away by herself.

When she came back, Father went skiing alone in the mountains.

The first Sunday that they all went out together again, there was a violent storm. The woodland paths were dripping wet, like Tina's and Tim's hair. There was a stormy atmosphere between Mother and Father, too. Mother's eyes were red with crying.

The first angry words were spoken. Tim and Tina hardly recognized their parents.

The time between storms grew shorter. One morning Tim and Tina's parents started shouting—or rather, yelling—at each other at the tops of their voices. Breakfast dishes went flying around the kitchen, and there was a lot of broken china on the floor. Terrified, Tim and Tina locked themselves in the bathroom and put their hands over their ears so they could not hear the shouting.

Then everything happened rather fast. No one asked Tim and Tina's opinion.

Mother packed Father's suitcases and put them outside the door, and Father went away. He found himself a small apartment.

Important-looking letters from lawyers kept coming for a whole year. Then the case of Fechner against Fechner was settled, and they were divorced.

Mother got custody of Tim and Tina Fechner, minors aged seven and eleven. Father could see the children twice a month, and they could stay with him for half of the school vacations.

When Father came to see the children, Mother went to her bedroom and did not come out again until she heard him leaving. Tim used to stay in her room with her. He didn't want to see Father, anyway.

Although it was not Father's fault.

Although it was not Mother's fault.

It was nobody's fault.

What happens is that when love dies, a great many people get hurt.

Father was very lonely. Only Tina stood by him, his own dear Tina.

TINA

"People can get used to anything."

I can't get that remark out of my head. Granny Fechner often makes it when she wants to calm herself down, and it's not true. Well, it is not true for me. I will never get used to seeing Father only twice a month. I will never get used to Mother disappearing into her room when he visits us.

I will never get used to the way nobody would even think of laughing on those weekends, and how doors seem to slam all by themselves. They can't stand the strain, either.

"I'm a bit early," says Father, sitting at the desk in my room waiting for me. It's his day to visit.

I stay in the doorway. I would really like to throw myself into his arms. But supposing Mother's door opens at just that moment and she gives me that disapproving look—"Oh, so you love him more than you love me"— then there'll be trouble. And I've had plenty of that for now, anyway. No more trouble, thanks.

"Where's Tim?" I ask. The words don't come out of my mouth the way I wanted, and I have to ask again. Father points to the door of Mother's room.

Now neither of us knows what to say. There's silence for a few moments.

"Well, and how's school these days, Tina?" asks Father briskly. He swallows. He looks sad, so sad that I . . . I kneel down in front of him and find myself crying, though I don't want to cry. Father ruffles my hair.

A drop of water lands on the back of my neck. So Father's crying, too. Mother comes out of her room with Tim trotting along behind her. I stand up and pretend nothing's wrong.

Mother has an unfriendly expression on her face. And suddenly Father is looking quite different, too, not at all nice anymore.

"I want to go to the movies with the children," he says.

"Fine, if the children want to go to the movies with *you* . . ." says Mother.

"I don't! I don't!" Tim plants himself in front of Father and glares crossly at him. "I want to stay with my Mommy!" He takes Mother's hand, for safety's sake. Coward!

"And I don't want to spend Christmas with you, either!"

Father meets Tim's eyes and won't look away. Tim is so embarrassed, he sticks out his tongue at Father.

"I'm coming with you, Father," I say quickly, and I go out of the room to get my coat.

When I come back, there's still silence in the room. A silence in which I can hear the angry things Mother and Father are saying to each other. Saying them in their minds as they face one another silently.

A silence in which thoughts can be read.

Now I'm sitting in the movies with Father. I am not at all interested in the movie; I expect I'll come out not having the faintest idea why the bearded man kissed the woman with the huge bosom and the bright green dress. Yuk!

Father is rustling his bag of popcorn. My fingers are sticky with licorice. I wipe my hand on the arm of my seat. It's a red velvet seat.

Time is passing very slowly. Why am I sitting here, anyway? I don't think I want to be here. I want to be with Father in his new apartment, cuddling with him, and turning on the television. I can't do that at home. Mother says too much television softens the brain. I want, I want, I want . . . Mother says I'm about the most self-centered girl in the world. I can't help it. Now and then I have tried to stop thinking about myself and think only unselfish thoughts, like loving your nearest and dearest and caring for your sick neighbor and so forth. But I've never had a sick neighbor, and I love my nearest and dearest, anyway—Mother and Father and Tim, I mean. Only . . . well, sometimes I'm not too sure if they care about that.

Oh, well. I'm a person, too. I'm important as well. I'm very, very important to myself. I come first. Then Mother and then Father and then Tim and then Cactus and Slow-and-Solid. Sometimes I change the order around. If I'm mad at all of them, Slow-and-Solid comes first. She never answers back.

Father scratches his nose. Then he picks it a bit. I smile and knock his elbow off the arm of his seat.

"Oh, dear!" says Father guiltily. He looks at me. "Are you bored?" he whispers. I nod in the dark, but he can see me nodding, the way I could see him picking his nose just now.

Father takes my arm and stands up. "Come on," he says. "Come on." We push our way along the row of seats. They're all full, and people mutter. That doesn't bother me, because Father bears the brunt of it. If I were alone I'd feel so embarrassed I'd want the ground to open and swallow me up. No, I probably would have sat there until the movie ended. I might even have gone to sleep. I'm good at going to sleep in the movies. I can even sleep holding on to the strap in the bus. Father always says he envies my ability to do that.

It's cold in Father's apartment, which is small and very comfortable, in spite of being cold. Father says that's because the previous tenant was a woman who lived there with three cats. So it's bound to be comfortable. I'd like to have a cat, too, but I can't, because cat hairs give Mother whooping cough or something like that—anyway, if she's near a cat she can't catch her breath and she turns white. Pity.

Father rubs his hands and lights the little gas fire. I lie on the nice soft rug, close my eyes, and wish Mother were here. Only if we were quite sure there wasn't a single cat hair left in the apartment, of course.

Father lights a cigarette. He's started smoking again since the divorce. I remember how they both gave up smoking together. There were jars of candy all over the place, and large packs of chewing gum, to help them shake off their craving for cigarettes. Tim and I were very pleased about it, because the cigarette smoke smelled so horrible.

Now Father is sitting on the bed, on a new bedspread I haven't seen before. It's a lovely one, patchwork in shades of red and pink and orange. Perhaps the woman with the three cats left it here.

4

"Does she cry a lot?" asks Father suddenly. He isn't looking at me, he's looking at the ceiling, watching smoke rings rise.

"Yes," I say, because it's true.

"How about you?" Father asks me.

"I'm all right," I say. I mean, what am I supposed to say? It isn't exactly a lie, either. There are days when I imagine, on my way home from school, that everything will be just the way it used to be. Father in his usual place, Mother in hers, Tim everywhere, Cactus on the sofa, Slow-and-Solid underneath the bureau.

Father goes into his little kitchen to make coffee. I stay sitting on the rug, feeling very sad. I wish I could crawl over the rug and underneath the door and turn into a puddle and flow slowly down the stairs. Drip, drip, drip . . .

ANGELICA

At the same moment Angelica, Tim and Tina's mother, is lying on her bed with a pillow over her head. If she peeks through the gap between the pillow and the bedspread, she can see Tim sitting on the edge of the bed. She would know he was sitting there even without seeing him, because he keeps kicking the bed frame without missing a beat and trying to whistle through the space in his teeth.

Angelica presses the pillow against both her ears and

shuts her eyes so tight she can see little colored stars twinkling in a dark sky. This helps her not to cry; she can feel tears welling up inside her and she doesn't want to let them out.

Plop. The pillow lands against the wall.

Tim stops whistling.

"Oh, Tim," says Angelica, putting her head in Tim's small lap. She is crying hard.

"Why are you crying?" asks Tim anxiously.

He knows why she is crying, but he doesn't know what else to say. Of course she is crying for exactly the same reason that he and Tina have often cried, and probably Father sometimes cries, too.

Tim looks as if he were thinking hard. Nothing is the way it ought to be.

"We're a very sad family," says Tim. He cannot understand why his mother suddenly takes his head in her hands, kisses him on the mouth, and laughs, sniffing up her tears at the same time and then wiping her eyes on his thigh, but he laughs, too.

"That will change, that will change," says Angelica, looking steadily into Tim's eyes. "It will change, darling, honestly it will." And the way Angelica says that, Tim has to believe her.

T I N A

It was a very boring Sunday afternoon with Father. We just couldn't think what to talk about. I wanted to tell Father how much I love him and how sad I am, but I simply couldn't say anything sensible, and neither could he. So instead of being nice to each other, we sat and watched television programs about Christmas for two hours. And I don't feel Christmassy, not in the least. Father didn't even notice when I turned the television off. He went on staring at the blank screen with his thoughts somewhere else. I wish I could read people's thoughts. I'm sure they'd be different from the things people say. But then again, perhaps our thoughts—Father's thoughts and mine—are so confused and mixed up that they wouldn't make sense, anyway. . . .

I've been sitting on the toilet for a long time. I like sitting on the toilet. It's my best place for thinking.

When was I as unhappy as I am now? I can't remember. The odd thing is that I'm not sad about being sad. I am just sad. I wonder if what Mother said is right? You can't be really happy unless you can be sad, too? Because there are no valleys without mountains, no winter without summer, no cold without heat, no sound without silence?

I will have to think about that a lot more. In fact I guess I'll have to spend the rest of my life in the bathroom. Mother can hand me my meals and a pillow and a blanket through the bathroom window. Then all I'll need is a few books and my cassette recorder with my favorite cassettes. There's one I especially like, by

Bettina Wegner; she's always so sad, too. I could do with an air mattress as well. I only measure four feet nine so our bathroom is long enough for me to lie down there. . . .

"Tina, I want to do a weewee!" squeals Tim, thumping on the door. So much for that! Too bad. He begrudges me just about everything. He knows perfectly well I like to spend a long time in the bathroom!

All the same, I say, "Coming!" I think I'm a wonderful big sister, I really am. Kind and understanding. Only just sometimes, like now, underneath all my kindness I imagine myself kicking his bottom hard with a big winter boot on. That feels good.

KARL

The telephone is ringing and ringing. Karl Fechner doesn't pick up the receiver. Odd how different the sound of a telephone can be, he thinks. Sometimes irritating, sometimes demanding, sometimes cheerful. And sometimes so deafening that it hurts, and he feels like picking up the whole thing and flinging it at the wall.

It would break to pieces, and they'd all be lying about the floor: the dial, the diaphragm, the bell, and the screws and wires.

Cautiously, Karl puts the telephone down on the table. It is still ringing. He can feel the sound deep inside him, making its way through his fingertips and into his body.

Karl swings around in his swivel chair. The weather is awful outside. The birch trees look as if something had been gnawing at them. He never could stand birch trees. The cars are covered with dirt and mud. A woman walks by. She does not look very cheerful, either, in her gray coat; her face is pinched and she walks fast.

Karl knows that you see only what you want to see. Grief goes with grief, gray goes with gray. His own grief keeps him from seeing the bright colors of the children's jackets; it is midday and they are coming out of school.

The laughter of the children does not come through his window. He wonders whether to get undressed again and go to bed to sleep away his troubles. He could make a big mug of cocoa, he could fill a hot-water bottle and put it on his stomach, he could take a book off the bookshelf, he could turn on the television, he could telephone friends, perhaps he could sit in the bathtub having a pine-fragrance foam bath and call them. None of these ideas really appeals to him.

Karl stands up and goes to the mirror. He fingers his mustache.

He has often been able to hide behind that mustache. No one could tell if the corners of Karl Fechner's mouth were turning up or down underneath it. Should he shave it off? Karl shrugs his shoulders. He does not like himself one bit today. He slams his right fist into the palm of his left hand.

"Oh, who cares?" Karl shouts at his reflection in the mirror, not that his reflection can do anything about it.

He goes back to his swivel chair and sits there brooding gloomily. Hours pass by. Hours and hours, and Karl sits motionless in his swivel chair until darkness falls.

T I N A

Mother has gone out. Gone to meet a friend she used to know; I've forgotten her name.

Tim and I are at home on our own. Tim is lying stretched out on the living room carpet, listening to his favorite record. I am in the kitchen, wondering whether to clear the things out of the dishwasher or not.

I'd rather not. The refrigerator is empty, and I'm hungry. Slow-and-Solid crawls out of her corner and across the kitchen floor.

"She's hungry, same as me!" says Tim. He comes into the kitchen, wriggling along on his tummy after Slow-and-Solid. At least the kitchen floor gets clean that way.

"Banana?" I ask.

Tim gets up on his knees and shakes his head. "Something that's right for tortoises," he says. He looks in the garbage and finds Slow-and-Solid a lettuce leaf.

There's no sausage left. No cheese, either.

"I hate this place!" I shout, slamming the refrigerator door. Tim bursts into laughter. It's nice when Tim laughs. His laughter's contagious, like measles. We laugh all the way to the living room, where the record is still running.

Cactus is rolling about on the carpet getting his fleas into its pile. He picked them up outdoors somewhere or other. Tim flings himself on Cactus, who runs away.

Tim takes my hand and we dance.

"Let's have waffles!" says Tim.

There's still some flour and two eggs in the back of the refrigerator, and half a quart of milk.

We make waffles, put lots of butter and jam on them, and gobble them up.

It's nice without Mother. It's nice without Father.

Tim wants to take a bath. I run water into the tub, and Tim squirts half a bottle of Blue Ocean Moisture Bath into it. We get undressed and play with our pirate ship; we capture an overloaded liner with lots of horrible people on board who hate children.

It's a wonderful evening. Tim wants to wash his hair, entirely of his own free will, and he looks sweet with a cap of soapy lather on his head. I suddenly love him so much I'd like to lick him all over, but Tim can't stand that sort of thing.

"Right!" he says, and he stands up and pees into the bathwater, making it arch a long way. I jump out of the tub and wrap myself in one of Mother's soft bath towels. Spluttering, Tim drops back into the warm, soapy water, rinses the lather off his head, and then gets out. He puts almost all the toothpaste in the tube on his toothbrush and then brushes the sugar from the waffles out of his little teeth. It's amazing, it's like a miracle! Tim's growing up.

"Well?" says Tim, showing me his gleaming white teeth.

"Great!" I tell him.

"Mommy, tuck me in bed!" squeaks Tim, clinging to me like a spider monkey.

I'll never be mad at Tim again about anything. I feel very good, putting his pajamas on him and reading him one more Winnie-the-Pooh story.

He soon falls asleep.

I look at Tim for a long time. He's lovely. He has Mother's long eyelashes and Father's light brown skin. He has blue eyes, same as me, and a dimple in his right cheek. I feel my own right cheek. There's a dimple there, too. My little brother. I daydream. Tim and I on a desert island. Just a palm tree on it, and maybe a cow to give us milk, and a baker's shop where we could buy bread and butter. A hut made of palm leaves, with a view of the sea, and the sea's full of fish who come up on land all ready to fry, maybe in a crispy breadcrumb coating. We could do with a Chinese take-out place, too, and possibly a small movie theater with a hundred and fifty cartoon films and Westerns. That's what I like; Tim likes fairy tales better.

There'd be no Mother there, and no Father, either.

And we wouldn't be sad anymore.

ANGELICA

Renate never showed up. Angelica Fechner is trying to calm herself down by stirring her coffee vigorously.

"Watch the cup, miss!" the bony-legged waitress tells her.

The man sitting at the next table clears his throat and moves a little closer.

"Upset about something?" he asks, smiling at Angelica in a way she does not like.

"No," she snaps. She wants to be left alone. She glares angrily at him. "No!" she snaps again.

The man raises his hands in a defensive gesture, and then picks up a newspaper to hide behind it.

Angelica pays for her coffee and leaves. She walks through the rain until her shoes are soaked and her body tired. When she feels she is about to cry she steps just inside the entrance of a building, rests her forehead against the wall, and lets the tears flow.

Then she feels better.

She is looking forward to getting home, to seeing Tim and Tina. Her children. Not until Angelica puts the key in the lock does she realize that she was looking forward to seeing Karl, too: It is his key, the one with the red mark on it.

She feels very cold. It is some time before she can pull herself together enough to open the door.

K A R L

Day is dawning, and Karl is still sitting in his swivel chair, asleep. The noise of the first garbage collectors wakes him abruptly. His throat hurts.

Karl groans. His eyes are swollen. Disgusted, he looks at the cigarette butts in the overflowing ashtray. The place stinks of cold smoke. Karl is freezing.

His wretched thoughts of the previous evening all come back to him, one after another. Worn out, he closes his eyes. For the first time he understands how people must feel when they don't want to go on living. A hopeless feeling. Cold, deep down inside.

He would like to go to sleep in his swivel chair and never wake up again. Or, no, he *would* like to wake up again, but not until his problems have solved themselves.

Karl sits up straight. Angry with himself for his stupid thoughts, he gets out of the chair and gives it a violent push. The chair falls over.

There's always some way out, there's always some way out. Karl goes to the closet and flings open the door. He turns on the radio. He wants to let some life into the place, life and noise. Music blares from the loudspeaker. Karl couldn't care less what the neighbors think. He knows what he wants to do now.

Carefully, he packs a suitcase.

He counts out three thousand dollars in traveler's checks on the desk, leafs through his savings book, and nods. It will be enough. He finds his passport in the desk drawer and nods again. It is still valid, and it covers both the children, too.

14

Karl gets the telephone book and looks up the numbers of several airlines that operate charter flights.

He pours himself a glass of brandy because he is shaking so much. He picks up the receiver.

When he starts speaking he realizes that his jaws hurt, and then discovers, for the first time, that his teeth have been clenched together ever since he woke up.

TINA

I'm the first to wake. That doesn't often happen. It's cold. I bet something is wrong with our decrepit heating system again. Cactus is lying on the end of Tim's bed, something Mother can't stand because of all the dog hairs in the laundry. Tim's asleep with his mouth open. His bottom is bare, and one pajama leg is hanging out of bed. I cover him up. Chilly, barefoot, and swearing quietly to myself, I go down to the basement, push the red knob on the boiler, and stand around shivering for a while. That really wakes me up. Going upstairs again, I open my eyes wide and fling my arms around to get warm.

And then I trip and fall.

This is a fine way for the day to begin. A day that starts like this can't end well, either. I don't want to go to school. I can't hear anything on the other side of the big bedroom door.

Mother must have earplugs in her ears. At least, nothing moves inside the room when I knock. Cautiously, I turn the door handle.

"Mother!" I rush around to the other side of the empty bed. Mother is lying there on the carpet. My heart is thumping frantically. Dead, dead, dead, it thumps. My mother's dead.

But Mother is not dead. She heaves a loud sigh when I shake her and mutters something I can't catch. I get angry and shout into her ear. Then she sits up and stares at me, with a look in her eyes I can't describe. As if I were a stranger.

Mother rolls up her eyes and drops back again. Only now do I see the bottle standing beside the bed. A bottle and a half-empty glass.

My mother smells like some awful old tramp.

"Drank . . . drank too much," Mother babbles. She sits up again and puts her arms around my neck. I'm kneeling in front of her, and her weight nearly pulls me over. I sway like a leaf blowing in the wind.

Leaning on my shoulder, Mother begins to cry. My nightgown gets all wet. Probably salty, too.

Oh, Mother, Mother. I stroke her, and the more I stroke her the more she cries.

Tim is standing in the doorway, wide-eyed, with Cactus behind him. When I make signs to Tim to go away they both obey. The loud sound of the toilet flushing drowns out Mother's sobs. She lets go of me and stares in horror at the alarm clock. "Seven-thirty!" she cries. She wipes away the last of her tears and goes off to join Tim in the bathroom.

When she leaves us outside school just before eight, she gives me a hug.

"Thank you, Tina," she says.

I don't say anything, but silently I'm calling Father all the worst names I can think of.

And I love him so much, all the same.

ANGELICA

"Goodness, what *do* you look like?"

Karin is laughing at Angelica—her tousled hair, the dark rings under her eyes, her skirt, which is on all crooked. "I don't feel too well," Angelica says. Her head hurts at every step she takes, it hurts right down to her teeth, even her hair hurts.

Unhappily, she looks at the two piles of books she has to process. Next to them lies a disorganized heap of index cards, reminder notes, Christmas cards, invitations to a reading, invoices: They all have to be filed. Her head hurts twice as much at the sight of them.

"Would you recommend this book for my grand-daughter, Mrs. Fechner?" asks Mr. Wippel, a retired chimney sweep.

"I haven't read it," says Angelica in a more unfriendly tone than she had intended.

Mr. Wippel is surprised. Mrs. Fechner is usually the soul of kindness. She can usually tell you all about the books!

But he only has to look at her: The way she looks now, nothing much can be expected of Angelica. "Won't anything bring you luck today—not even a chimney sweep crossing your path?" he asks her quietly.

She almost bursts into tears again. "No, I don't think so," she says in a stifled voice; she blows her nose on a large handkerchief and tries to smile. "Sorry, Mr. Wippel."

"Ah, men are no good," he says.

"Mine is," Angelica hears herself say, to her own surprise, and then she turns around and runs to the ladies' room, where she locks the door and spends the next ten minutes trying to calm down again.

Angelica cries and hammers at the mirror with her hands. She is so unhappy she would like to tear the sink right out of the wall.

K A R L

Ten to two. Karl has been constantly looking at his watch for the last ten minutes, but time will not be hurried along. His feet are freezing; the first snow has fallen. It is really beginning to look like Christmas.

Karl shifts impatiently from one foot to the other. He is as tense as a bowstring.

The black canvas bag, crammed full, is standing in

the snow between Karl's legs. An hour ago, kneeling on the floor of the store and half deafened by the sound of Christmas carols, Karl had stuffed two sets of girls' underclothes into it, and two sweaters and two pairs of pants, all Tina's size.

Karl closes his eyes and feels the blood burning in his eyelids. He blinks. A few children are trickling out through the school gates. More and more come, until a wide stream is pouring out into the open: a stream made up of laughing faces, waving arms, hopping legs, brightly colored school bags.

Legs apart, Karl stands there with his arms folded.

Tina sees him at once. She runs to him, laughing. But when she stops in front of her father she is serious again; in her mind's eye, she can see her mother lying on the carpet, drunk and unhappy.

"Hello," says Karl.

"Mother's been drinking, all because of you!" Tina shouts. For a moment Karl looks down at the ground, not sure whether to reply. He takes Tina gently by the arm.

"Tina, I'm going away," he says.

"Have fun!" growls Tina, and then, curiously, she asks, "Where are you going?" For the first time she notices the black canvas bag.

"Somewhere warm," says Karl, turning up the collar of his jacket. "Where the sea is blue, and no one will argue with me. The plane leaves in an hour and a half."

"What, before Christmas?" says Tina. She herself does not know why this idea horrifies her so much.

Karl does not answer her question. Instead, he asks, "Will you come to the airport with me?" And when Tina hesitates, he begs, "Please, Tina dear."

Tina nods. Her mouth is full of saliva; she takes a deep breath and spits. It goes at least six feet.

"Not bad," says Karl, "if not very ladylike!"

Tina laughs, takes her father's arm, and forgets her sadness for a moment. It's nearly always like that: Karl just has to say something funny and everything looks different. But it never lasts long.

"See you!" calls Rainer Vogt, who sits next to Tina in school, as he gets into his mother's car.

"See you!" Tina waves.

Karl hails a taxi, heaves the black canvas bag inside, pushes Tina in after it, and sits beside the driver.

"The airport," he says. The driver nods, sets the meter, checks the traffic in the rearview mirror, and starts off. Tina is sucking a lollipop she had stuck between the pages of her history book and does not say a word the whole way.

T I N A

Ouch. The lollipop got stuck in my teeth.

Now it's stuck to the taxi seat. The driver hasn't noticed; he's looking straight ahead. I lean forward and tickle Father's neck.

"Don't!" says Father, turning around to look at me, his lips pressed together in such a funny way.

"You don't need to be sad anymore," I tell him. "You're going away."

But my words are left hanging in the air, because Father doesn't reply, and the taxi driver is taking the access ramp to the airport very fast, so that I'm thrown against the door.

The place smells of fuel. I like the smell; I breathe it in deeply. It makes me feel a bit dizzy.

Carefully, Father unfolds a ten-dollar bill and watches it disappear into the taxi driver's wallet. When I see Father standing there with that sad look in his eyes, the black canvas bag over his shoulder, bending forward slightly and with his hair a bit messy, I think he's great! I suddenly feel I love him so much I could bite him, but I don't.

Better not think about him going away. What sort of a Christmas will we have without him? I can't imagine it. Suppose he stays away for good? I never thought of that before, and it terrifies me.

"Aren't you ever going to come back?" I tug at Father's sweater.

Why doesn't he answer? He just swallows in that peculiar way, like he did just now. With his Adam's apple jerking up and down. I take Father's hand. It's icy cold and a bit damp. What's the matter? I realize Father is trembling.

"Oh, yes," says Father, letting go of my hand again.

I stumble after him through the automatic doors of the airport. It's warm inside the building. I fool around with the doors a couple more times, making them open and close for nothing. I can't stand those doors, I don't know why, but they always annoy me whenever I'm at the airport. And I come to the airport quite often, because Grandma visits us once a month.

I have trouble catching up with Father. He's heading for a desk with a long line of people in front of it. We don't say a word to each other until he's reached it. He puts the black bag on the conveyor belt, and the woman at the desk asks me to take my foot off the belt, because that's where the baggage is weighed.

"Or do you want to pay for excess baggage?" she adds.

I shake my head. The bag disappears behind a curtain made of dark leather straps. I'd love to go off on the conveyor belt, too. The woman would say, "Excess baggage," and then she'd put a number around my wrist and stick a green label across my mouth, slap the soles of my feet, and off I'd go, through the curtain and into the dark, then onto the truck with the rest of the baggage, and finally into the hold of the plane, in among all the bags and suitcases.

No, maybe not. I guess I'd probably get squashed.

"Good-bye, Daddy," I say as we're moved on from the check-in desk to the line for customs. I've got to see that I get out of the line in time, and catch the next airport bus back home. Mother will be expecting me; so will Tim.

But suddenly Father says, "You can come into the departure lounge with me!" He puts his ticket, and another one, too—no, it must be a baggage claim check or something like that—away in his jacket pocket.

We're standing at a sort of green shelter, with a policeman sitting in it really high up, behind a glass window, to inspect passports. He's so high up I can only see his hat and his eyes and his nose. His eyes look hard at Father and then at me. I grin. The eyes smile back. Father lets out a deep breath and coughs.

"All right," says the policeman.

Father's holding my hand so tight my fingers hurt.

"But I've got to go now," I protest as he draws me on with him toward the tunnel leading to the plane. I can smell that he's sweating.

"Father," I say out loud, once more. Father gives me a look that leaves me speechless. I can only repeat, "Father," softly this time, and then I'm in the middle of a pushing, shoving crowd of people hurrying down the sloping tunnel. I can see a metal opening ahead of me. The door of the plane. The engines are running. I feel hot, I can hardly breathe, my school bag sticks out at an angle and makes me and two people behind me stumble. They give me dirty looks. Father's gone, no, he hasn't, he's back again, right behind me. We're in the plane. Father pushes me into an empty row of seats.

I'm sitting by a window. I'm going to be sick; if something doesn't happen soon I'll throw up, I bet I will! I take a deep breath, and I don't feel sick anymore.

I can't speak, though. My words have all gone, along with the sick feeling. I'll be dumb for the rest of my life.

Father drops into the seat beside me, turns to me,

takes my head and buries it in his lap. I can feel his warm breath close to my ear.

"Darling," Father whispers, "darling, don't be angry, don't scream, stay with me." He's crying quietly and looking out of the window so that nobody will notice.

I feel a sob in my chest, and then I'm crying, too. I don't think I'll ever stop.

"When we arrive we'll call Mother right away," Father whispers in my ear. "Really we will—I promise you!"

My tears have dried up.

The plane starts moving. Father fastens my seat belt carefully and drops kisses on my nose and my cheeks.

"You're crazy, Father," I say all of a sudden.

I didn't know a person could laugh sadly, but that's what Father does now.

When we take off I'm pressed back in my seat. Then we're up in the air, and *whoosh!* we go up through the clouds. It's blue, everything is sky-blue.

I'm crazy, too. I must be out of my mind! Why else would I be feeling so happy?

There's a sign over the window saying EMERGENCY EXIT. Suppose I just opened the emergency exit and walked out onto the clouds there? Let myself fall into those fluffy clouds and snuggle down. Forget about everything.

There's a little bottle of wine and two glasses on Father's table. He pours it out and hands me one of the glasses. It smells like sparkling mineral water, only sour.

"Children aren't allowed to drink alcohol," I tell Father.

"I never was much of a father," he says, raising his glass. So I take a big gulp, too, and make a face.

"Yuk," I say, pouring the rest of my wine into his glass. I'd rather have mineral water.

My father's kidnapping me. It's crazy. Absolutely crazy. I'm giggling; I'm all mixed up. Father looks at me doubtfully. "Are you feeling all right?" he asks. I shake my head and nod at the same time. How I can do that I don't know, but it works.

ANGELICA

Angelica is storming around the house, flinging open all the doors, tearing the bedclothes off Tina's bed; she almost steps on Slow-and-Solid; she even opens the door of the refrigerator and slams it shut again at once.

"Where's Tina?" she shouts at Tim.

Tim sits there, small and trembling, in front of the half-completed Christmas star he is making out of straws, clinging anxiously to his chair. Helplessly, he shrugs his shoulders. He might as well be asking his mother, "Where's Tina?" Tina is not there. She didn't come home from school, it is five o'clock, and she's three and a half hours late.

"If he's *done* it . . ." gasps Angelica, "if he's *done* it . . ." She doesn't finish her sentence and doesn't need to. Tim knows she means Father. And the threat he made when he said, once, how he didn't get nearly enough time, and if something wasn't done about it he would simply go away with Tina. A long way away.

"Oh, Timmy," says Angelica, suddenly all soft again. She takes her son in her arms, kisses him, and cries over him.

Tim pushes her away. "Got a tummyache," he mutters. He sweeps the straw star onto the carpet and goes to bed, all by himself. Angelica, thunderstruck, watches him go. She wipes her tears away and goes to the telephone. She dials three times before she gets through to the school office, and they don't know anything there. There is a list of the children in Tina's class, in alphabetical order, hanging over the telephone. Angelica dials the first number. She can't be polite. Several times she just crashes the receiver down again after a few seconds. Until she gets to the letter *V*, and Rainer Vogt. "Oh, her father came to get her," he says.

"On foot or by car?" Angelica's questions hammer at the helpless Rainer. He calls his mother.

"Is something wrong, Mrs. Fechner?"

"Tina's disappeared. Rainer was just telling me my husband took her."

"Oh, yes—we saw them. Mr. Fechner hailed a taxi. I was just about to ask if I could give him and Tina a lift anywhere, but it looked as if he was going away, isn't that right?"

"How do you know?" asks Angelica.

"He had a big travel bag with him. I was quite surprised, because the Christmas vacation doesn't begin till next week! Is anything the matter?"

"He simply took my daughter along with him," says Angelica, stunned.

"What, in the middle of the school year?" Mrs. Vogt sniffs a scandal.

"We're divorced," says Angelica, almost whispering. She does not want to go on talking to this woman, whom she hardly knows.

"I see," says Mrs. Vogt. She apologizes for having to cut the conversation short, but she really must go now. A divorce is so common these days, the details are no longer interesting.

"Good luck," says Mrs. Vogt, promptly hanging up. Angelica feels a huge lump in her throat. She swallows and swallows, but it won't go away. She makes herself some coffee. I mustn't break down, I simply must not break down. She summons up all her strength.

Angelica has drunk her coffee and calmed down a little. She goes into Tim's room. Tim only nods when she tells him, "Don't go out of the house, don't go near the stove, leave the windows closed, and don't answer the door to any strangers."

It is not much good relying on Cactus to bark; he is no use as a watchdog. He rubs against Angelica's knee, and she absentmindedly pats him.

Tim pulls the bedclothes up over his head.

"Did you hear what I said?" Angelica asks the small figure under the sheets.

"Yes," says a hollow voice from under them. Tim likes his cave. All he wants is to be left in peace there, to listen to cassettes of fairy tales until they lull him to sleep.

Angelica sighs, puts on her coat, and goes out.

Tim becomes one of the three little pigs and closes

the door of his house. Cactus, the big bad wolf, sits helplessly by the bed with his tongue hanging out. His bowl of water is empty. No one is taking care of him. Feeling hurt, Cactus gets underneath Tim's bed. Slow-and-Solid moves off to the left and goes into a corner. Everything is very quiet. Click. Tim switches on the fairy tales and closes his eyes.

K A R L

Karl Fechner is tipsy. After seven small bottles of wine, he is looking around him in a friendly way and feeling very tired. Tina has been asleep for the last hour, curled up in a ball with her head on Karl's lap.

He feels safe here, surrounded by cheerful people flying off to spend Christmas in the sun, alone or with their families. Then, three weeks later, they'll be flying home again, tanned and rested.

Karl laughs out loud. Who knows what he will be doing in three weeks' time?

"No home now," mutters Karl.

"What did you say?" The elderly lady on Karl's left, interested, turns her head closer to him.

"Oh, nothing." Only now does Karl realize he was thinking out loud.

"Your daughter?" inquires the lady, looking curiously at Karl. He nods, but assures himself he has no intention of entering into a conversation. "Yes," he says.

The lady shrugs her shoulders and turns back to her magazine.

Gently, Karl strokes Tina's hair. The same color as his own. If he put his hair down on Tina's, nobody could tell where his began or hers left off.

She has Angelica's nose. A snub nose, but a very determined one all the same. His dimples; both children have inherited them from him.

Tina is sleeping with her mouth open. She is snoring a little, she may catch a cold.

"The fresh air will be good for her," says Karl suddenly to the lady sitting next to him.

Pleased that he has given in, she says, "Yes, and for me, too. I have asthma, you know!"

He set the trap for himself, and now he has fallen into it. Resigned, he listens as the lady tells him her life story.

ANGELICA

"Kidnapped? How do you mean, kidnapped?"

The policeman is not very friendly and would much rather have nothing to do with this case.

Angelica is trying hard to keep calm: not easy when you are trembling and quivering all over.

"We're divorced," she says, "but *I* have care and custody."

The policeman looks suspiciously at Angelica.

"Do you think I'm making all this up or what?" she cries indignantly, clutching the back of the chair.

He does not reply but turns slowly toward his typewriter. Deliberately, he feeds a sheet of paper into it, raises one eyebrow, and asks, "Name? Age? Kidnapped where? Taken where?"

Angelica wonders why everything always happens at once. She does not believe in Fate, but she really would like to know why God (always supposing God exists) should allow this policeman to come her way, as well as all the rest of it.

"I should hope you would improve your attitude," says Angelica sharply, "or I will have to report you."

She hates threatening. What good does it do, anyway? She might perhaps get him to stop being nasty with her—an insignificant person coming in with a complaint—but would forcing him to turn his annoyance on his superior officer, who really could make trouble for him, make him cooperative?

At the moment, the answer, unfortunately, is yes. The policeman mutters something into his typewriter, calms down a bit, and says, sighing, "You wouldn't believe how hard it is, seeing nothing but angry faces all day!"

Exhausted, Angelica closes her eyes. If only she could be in a nice soft bed, have coffee brought to her, today's newspaper, a little hugging and petting, Tina's voice outside the door.

Here in the police station, Angelica reels off the required information. Child's age, height, weight, clothing, when last seen, was her husband ever violent . . .

At this she laughs bitterly. "Not him! He wouldn't

hurt a fly. He doesn't let anything bother him, not even if you smash the china; just says, 'Dear, dear!' and shakes his head."

"I see," says the policeman, frowning. Angelica thinks he looks stupid, but that may just be the mood she's in today. On the other hand, he really could be stupid, she tells herself.

"Well, now," says the policeman cautiously, looking at her nervously, "I tell you how it looks to me: could be that a nice fellow like that—wouldn't hurt his own child, I mean—and suppose he just wants a little time with her, well . . . er . . . I mean, school's not that much fun, ha ha!" He is becoming confused, because the anger in Angelica's face has him rattled. "I mean, Christmas, and maybe he wants a bit of peace and . . . er . . . "

This takes Angelica's breath away. "But she's *my* child!" she cries, once she is able to speak again. "He's got no right to do a thing like that to me!"

The policeman forces an official expression back on his face. "Well, everything will take its due course," he says, taking his form out of the typewriter. His finger runs along the lines of type on the sheet of paper. "Sign here, please!"

As Angelica goes down the steps and out into the snow, she knows why she was so furious: because the policeman just might have been right. Because it was possible that now, at this moment, Tina was happier than if she had been at home. So which of them did Tina belong to? Herself? Karl?

Tina doesn't belong to anyone but herself.

"Everything will take its due course," mutters Angelica.

Her limbs feel heavy as lead when she gets home, limply kisses Tim, and asks him to make her some coffee.

She takes the telephone to her bedside and crawls into bed. "Being in bed is great, isn't it, Mommy?" says Tim, slipping in beside her and snuggling into her arms. Cactus licks Angelica's face with his big, doggy tongue.

T I N A

I never woke up in a plane before. Well, that's not surprising: I never went to sleep in a plane before. There's a loud noise in my ears. I dreamed of something, but I can't remember what. My dream has gone: probably disappeared under my seat and rolled forward now that we're coming in to land. Perhaps the captain of the plane is standing on my dream at this very moment and doesn't know it.

Not that reality's bad, especially not this reality. When I press my nose to the window I can see blue sea down below, and white bays, and far off there's something bright green, a forest.

I wish you wouldn't look at me in that worried way, Father. I'm fine. I'm not angry with you.

The woman sitting beside Father has closed her eyes, and her lips are pressed tight together as if she had a lemon in her mouth. I think she's afraid of landing. I can't see why people are afraid of coming closer to the ground.

Mother is terribly afraid of flying. In an airplane, she keeps going to the bathroom, drinking cup after cup of coffee, and getting more nervous the whole time. It's not until we've landed that she turns kind and nice again and acts as if nothing had been wrong. Mother.

I tug at Father's sleeve. "Have you got money for the telephone?" I ask. Father shakes his head. He is chewing gum, to stop his ears popping. "But we'll get some," he says. I feel a bit better.

Oops! An air pocket. And now we're down.

"Ladies and gentlemen, we have just landed at Tenerife Airport. Will you please remain in your seats until . . ."

Tenerife! How come I never thought of asking where we were flying, not until this minute? Oh, this will be wonderful, really wonderful! We went to Tenerife once before, when I was little and Tim was still a baby. We splashed around in the sea and got sand in between our toes and in our sandwiches.

It's hard to imagine how cold it must be at home. It's hard to imagine anything at home going on the same as before. Not for me, I mean, for the others. Annegret, for example, who's probably taking her bath now because she always has to go to bed about this time—it's eight o'clock. And Rainer is most likely watching television in his pajamas. And Linni will be sitting up slaving over her homework.

But I'm here! I've just landed in the warmth of an island far from home—it's even warm at night!

I keep close to Father as we go to pick up our baggage.

It seems like years before the black canvas bag finally comes around the corner on the conveyor belt. And it takes ages to get hold of the money we need for the telephone. Mother won't be mad when I tell her how warm it is here.

The telephone is ringing so far away. It only rings twice before Mother answers. "Mother," I say. I want to tell her how much I like it here, but Mother cries, "Oh, Tina, Tina, darling!" and I can't say another word. Father takes the receiver out of my hand. "Angelica," he says, "she's quite all right, and she came of her own free will, and . . ."

I can't quite make out what Mother is saying at the other end of the line, but I can tell that she's shouting.

"I can't tell you where we are," says Father. He is red in the face, and he's leaning on me, because he is trembling. "Angelica, no—please, Angelica . . ."

Then, quite suddenly, he hangs up.

"She's told the police," he says, and looks sadly around the large and almost empty airport building.

But why? I don't get it. After all, we called as soon as we arrived, didn't we?

"I guess now she'll tell the police everything's all right," I tell Father, but he shakes his head.

"They'll send me to jail," he mutters.

I shake my head. What nonsense! You can't get sent to jail just for going on vacation. All right, so we didn't really go on vacation in the usual way, making preparations and packing and so on, but we're on vacation all the same. If they send Father to jail they'll have to send me to jail, too. I tell him so, right away. "I'll go to jail with you," I say, "because it's just silly!"

Father's eyes look very sad. "All I'm allowed to do is pay money," he says. "I have no rights to my own daughter."

"You could have asked Mother to let me come," I say, a bit helplessly, and Father smiles the same odd, sad smile, runs his fingers through my hair, and then says, "Well, let's get moving." We board a bus which smells quite different from the buses at home. It soon starts off.

"The boat doesn't leave till tomorrow morning," says Father.

"Where are we going to sleep?" I ask, putting my feet on the black bag.

Father shrugs his shoulders. "We'll see."

Just at the moment I find I'm thinking rather a lot about Mother and Tim and Cactus and Slow-and-Solid, too—I hope Mother won't forget to feed Slow-and-Solid—and so I don't ask any more questions about this boat, and where it's taking us.

I don't do that till later.

KARL

Karl Fechner is staring out of the bus window into the darkness. So there he is with his daughter, Tina, who didn't really want to come along. Is she happy now?

Is he happy? He steals a sideways glance at Tina. She looks quite relaxed, peering bright-eyed out into the dark and smiling slightly to herself.

He is a criminal now. A law-breaker. The police could come any time and take him in. Name? Nationality? They could produce a long list from their pockets, and the name of Karl-Heinz Fechner would be somewhere on it. At least, perhaps it wouldn't be quite so soon. Perhaps the international police didn't know about the kidnapping yet. Perhaps Angelica was only bluffing and hadn't been to the police at all. Can you be jailed for kidnapping a child? If it's your own child? I'll have to go by an assumed name, thinks Karl. How do you do that sort of thing? In thrillers, every small-time crook knows where to get a false passport. A new passport, a new name, and off to South America with Tina to begin a new life.

"I'm not God Almighty," murmurs Karl to his conscience. "Tina loves Angelica, too, not just me." Only a few hours have passed, and the first doubts are already setting in: Did he do right?

"Oh, look, Father, look!" Tina presses her face to the window. The bus is passing through a small town and stops at the one set of traffic lights. There is a rickety wooden cart by the crossroads, piled high with cages containing animals. Rabbits, Siamese cats, birds, guinea pigs, rats, white mice . . . the lights change to green far too soon.

Karl's gloomy thoughts have been swept away. A little later the bus turns into a lively street. A crowd of people is moving past the restaurants and souvenir shops, which are still open. It is warm out. The bus stops. Karl and Tina let themselves be swept along to the door. Then they find themselves by the docks. At the sight and smell of the Atlantic, father and daughter stand there hand in hand, entranced.

A N G E L I C A

Angelica is feeling sick, very sick. As if she had leaden weights on her feet that keep her from getting up. Cactus is panting loudly. A regular squeaking noise comes from the children's room. Today Angelica couldn't care less whether Tim ruins the bedsprings or not.

Angelica listens to her body. "Be quiet!" she snaps at Cactus. The least little sound gets on her nerves today. The dog does stop panting. Angelica's stomach feels empty.

A memory comes back to her, a memory over ten years old: the day after Tina was born. That strange mixture of joy and a feeling of being deserted. Her empty stomach, and the child in her arms, which was no longer all her own, but belonged to itself.

It was quite different with Tim. She knew what was coming then.

Angelica had never thought what it might be like to have her daughter leave her at this age. Obviously, when they are eighteen, nineteen, twenty, children leave home. That is how it should be; it is good and right that way.

As a mother, Angelica would not be needed anymore. But that wouldn't be so bad: She would still be Angelica the librarian, and Angelica the woman herself.

Tina's only eleven, thinks Angelica. She still needs me. I need her, too.

Angelica bites the pillow, always a good means of stopping yourself from screaming. She doesn't want Tim to come in now and see her so sad. He is very cheerful just now. Almost as if he didn't care about his sister. Heartless little monster. Or maybe it's good for him to be on his own with me, thinks Angelica.

Angelica feels a surge of affection for Tim, her baby. It makes her throw back the bedclothes and get up. She leaves her sadness there in the bed.

"Hell," she mutters later, in the bathroom, trying to squeeze into her jeans. The zipper won't go up. Tim stands there laughing. "Mommy's getting fat," he says.

Angelica gives him a dirty look. "Idiot!" she says, then ruffles his hair and hugs him tight until he is struggling for air.

"I did it forty times!" says Tim breathlessly.

"Did what forty times?" A seam needs sewing on Angelica's black slacks; she picks up another pair.

"My trampoline jump," says Tim. "I did it for Tina. Now I know she'll be back soon, for sure."

Angelica is touched, but doesn't want to show it, not now. Her green slacks are all right. She still doesn't feel well. Silently, Slow-and-Solid crawls under the bureau in the hall.

In her mind, Angelica slips in under the tortoise shell, too, and stays there all day without coming out.

TINA

I've never seen so many dogs all together before. A pack of dogs! I laugh and laugh, and Father laughs, too. His sad face, the one he had just now, has fallen into the water. "Look, there goes my face!" he called. And it really did look as if a mask with two eyes and a sad mouth were floating in the water, in between waves.

A yellow dog suddenly rubs against my leg. Really yellow: not sunshine yellow, but something like the color of an unripe lemon. He isn't particularly good-looking but he has nice eyes, nice eyes like Tim's when Tim . . . I don't want to think about home just now. Go away, thoughts, go away. Go into the water. The dog sits down beside me.

A shadow looms up behind the little fishing boats. A huge shadow. Goodness, what a big ship! "That'll be it," says Father.

We watch intently as the ship comes closer to the dock, moving at a snail's pace, as it stops and then lies there quietly, opening its huge mouth with a squeal. Engines are started up, and then cars, construction machinery, trucks, motorcycles, and tractors come pouring out of the ship's hold.

People are crowding down into the harbor, climbing down some steps, which look really tiny. Many of them have huge backpacks with sleeping bags strapped on top. There are toddlers with tired eyes in the arms of their plump mothers, babies in slings and strollers. Men carrying cardboard cartons tied up with string, or balancing them on their heads. Men whose trousers, worn without suspenders, are nearly slipping off over their hips as they walk. And all wearing shiny, polished shoes.

"You can tell the tourists by their dirty shoes," says a voice near us.

It belongs to a young woman—no, more like a girl—or do I mean a woman after all? Well, anyway, she has a baby, too, carried in a sling around her, and a colored headscarf and sneakers covered with dirt. "It rained on the beach," she says, noticing my eyes resting on them. I feel a bit embarrassed.

"Have you been here long?" asks Father.

"Mm, quite a while, I suppose," she says. "I'm Inge and this is Anna."

"How do you do?" says Father, shifting from one foot to the other.

"And I'm Karl-Heinz Fechner," he introduces himself. He hesitates, swallows, and then goes on. "This is my daughter, Tina."

"But nobody ever calls Father Karl-Heinz, just Karl," I say. "Karl-Heinz is too long. I think it sounds silly."

"I like just Karl better, too," says Inge.

"Well then, Mrs. er . . ." says Father, fishing for her surname.

"Just Inge," says Inge. "You're just Karl and I'm just Inge!"

Father laughs. "A woman after my own heart," he says.

Baby Anna blinks for a moment, lets out a little yell, and stops it at once when Inge rocks her by taking a couple of steps. "Like a lamb!" I say, and Inge nods.

"Rocking soothes her," she says, and beckons to us. "Come on!"

I'm surprised to see how obediently Father puts the black bag over his shoulder and trots along after Inge. So I have to go, too.

It's soft underfoot: We're on the sandy beach. Only now do I notice little groups of people standing, lying, or sitting about the beach itself.

"Got somewhere to sleep yet?" asks Inge.

Father shakes his head. "We were thinking we might find a small hotel or something," he says.

Inge raises her eyebrows. "At this time of night? Not likely!"

But I'm tired. As I suddenly realize.

We've come to a sleeping bag spread out on the ground. There's one of those huge orange backpacks on top of it.

"Thanks," says Inge to a young man who stands up to make way for her.

"Got another cigarette?" he asks her.

Inge searches one pocket of the backpack and brings out a full pack. "Here," she says. "I'm trying to quit, anyway."

The young man grins, blinks, and goes off.

"Was that your husband?" I ask Inge.

"No, I don't know him," she says. "He was just keeping an eye on my things while I went to see who was coming off the ferry."

"That's a very rash sort of thing to do," says Father, shaking his head disapprovingly.

"Not when you know who you can trust," says Inge.

I'm getting more and more tired. Right now I wish I could be hanging in front of Mother's breast, just like baby Anna. It would be all warm and soft and cozy there, and I could have a lovely nap.

We sit down, and I curl up in Father's lap. He takes a sleeping bag out of our black canvas bag and covers me up with it. Inge kisses me on the forehead.

"Sleep well—we're off to Gomera tomorrow," she says. I'm so tired I feel a little dizzy. Gomera . . . that's a nice word. Anything that sounds so nice must be nice.

"Good night, Father," I murmur. "Good night, Mother, good night, Tim . . ."

KARL

So there they sit opposite each other, each with a sleeping child pressed close. Karl looks in amazement at baby Anna's peaceful face. He simply cannot remember now, what Tina looked like when she was as small as that. Just eleven years ago, but it might be centuries. Eleven years of making mistake after mistake. Eleven years of always looking forward to what the future might bring—more money, more comfort, and less and less time for living here and now.

Karl realizes his thoughts are going down dangerous paths. He does not want to be sad again. . . .

"You're not in a very good mood, are you?" Inge hands him a bottle of wine. He drinks some.

"Oh, I'm all right," he says. He would like to tell Inge all about it.

The wine is too warm, and tastes acid as it goes down his throat to his stomach, but at the same time it clouds his troubles.

"But I can see you're not," Inge insists. "It's all right, you can tell me about your problems. We're ships that pass in the night, we may never meet again."

Karl drinks some more wine; it is no better this time.

"The usual," says Karl, avoiding Inge's direct gaze.

"Trouble with her mother?" Inge looks at the sleeping Tina.

"We've been divorced for some time," says Karl quickly, feeling he has already said too much, which is nonsense. Divorced people, unfortunately, don't always think clearly.

Inge smiles. "Something that can't happen to me!" she says.

"It can happen to anyone," says Karl. "Perhaps you're too young to—"

"Nonsense." Inge interrupts him. "I'm thirty-two. I would say you were . . ." Inge licks her lips with the tip of her tongue. "I'd say you were about thirty-five."

"Thirty-seven," says Karl.

Inge shrugs her shoulders. "Well, anyway, there's not much age difference. I couldn't find myself in your sort of trouble because I don't plan to set up housekeeping again."

Karl is confused.

"I don't see Anna's father anymore," Inge explains.

"You quarreled?"

Inge shakes her head. "Well, no. I wanted a child, and Hans was very nice. He doesn't know he's a father." Inge chuckles and reaches for the bottle again, then says to herself, "No, Inge, no more wine. I'm still feeding Anna—don't want my baby to get drunk!"

"Suppose she asks about her father someday?" Karl is a little shocked; he thinks one shouldn't take life so lightly.

"It's better to have no father than a bad father," says Inge briefly. "I'll make sure Anna and I have plenty of friends."

Anna begins to cry. Inge pushes up her sweater and puts the baby to her breast. Anna sucks greedily.

"She feels happy with me," says Inge. "Isn't that enough? And I love her."

"Yes," says Karl, rather depressed. "It probably is enough." He is thinking along much the same lines as Tina, an hour before: how nice to be a baby again, cuddled to a soft breast, and go to sleep feeling happy and content. He thinks of his mother. He hasn't been to see her for two months.

Karl caresses Tina.

Anna has fallen asleep. Inge carefully settles her baby down beside her. It is getting cool; it must be after midnight. Karl's watch has stopped.

"Good night," says Inge, lying down and closing her eyes.

"Good night," says Karl. He won't be able to get to sleep now. He stays sitting there for a long time, not moving but staring at the stars, which look so much closer to the earth here, almost on the equator.

Only when the sky begins to get light on the horizon, and Karl realizes his fingers are numb, does he lie down, cover himself up, and fall asleep at once, with Tina's head in the crook of his arm.

ANGELICA

Angelica goes slowly downstairs, her footsteps echoing loudly through the old stairwell.

She can hardly believe what the lawyer said. "Your chances are slim, Mrs. Fechner. The law gives the parent who does not have custody the right to six and a half weeks' vacation with the child of the marriage. And the courts don't impose very severe penalties for causing a child to miss part of the school term these days. A fine, maybe. We can talk about it again in seven weeks' time."

At that Angelica had stood up and shouted angrily, "And suppose he's gone away for good with my daughter? To South America or somewhere?"

The lawyer had merely smiled and tried to calm her down. A horrible smile that was not a real smile at all, just a baring of the teeth, as false as his teeth themselves. Angelica hated him. First the policeman, then this lawyer . . .

"I don't suppose you have any children!" she had

shouted as she left, and he had leaned back in his chair and stared at her.

"No, Mrs. Fechner, I have spared myself that pleasure."

Now Angelica is out in the street. The air is cold and clear, the Christmas decorations have been up in the streets for some time. Angelica gets on a bus, battling with her tears. Not until a man in a hat asks her, two stops farther on, "Can I see your ticket, please?" does she realize that she has not bought one, and now she will have to pay a fine.

She hands over fifteen dollars almost without minding, although it is a good deal of money to her, just before Christmas. The other passengers, who of course all have their tickets, are watching.

"It's quite a risk, dodging the fare, young lady," says a man in a gray hat.

This is the last straw. "Oh, the hell with this rotten city!" Angelica snaps.

"You can always go somewhere else if you don't like it here," says the man. Fortunately, Angelica has to get out at this point.

TINA

"Stop it, Cactus!"

I push the dog's soft coat away from me and rub my eyes. Suddenly they are full of sand.

It isn't Cactus after all. It's that yellow dog I saw yesterday evening. Suddenly I feel very odd.

Mommy!

"Don't cry, Tina." Father is there, rocking me in his arms. The feeling of wanting to cry soon goes away, and I'm happy again. Only it was such a funny way to wake up, when I was dreaming of being at home.

I can't put the pieces of my dream back together. Something about Cactus, and Tim riding on his back, and Slow-and-Solid had wings . . .

"Good morning," says Inge.

"Doesn't she bite you?" I ask, rather alarmed, because it looks as if baby Anna is trying to eat Inge's breast and Inge.

Inge shakes her head.

"I'll get us something to eat from over there." Father points to a snack bar beyond the beach.

Watching him go away, his back turned to me, I feel scared. Suppose he doesn't come back? But I can see him all right, I can see him standing there, his turn comes, he is saying something, getting money out of his wallet, and then he comes back with his hands full.

He's bought delicious, huge, crusty rolls, with generous slices of cheese and ham inside them. I realize I'm starving. I eat two enormous rolls, Father can only manage one, and Inge just nibbles at hers, but she drinks half a quart of milk at one time.

There are sleeping bags all around us. Heads are looking out of many of them, and there's one over there with a man just crawling out of it—a man who's so tall and thin he looks as if he will never come to an end. A girl is playing a guitar and singing, but so badly out of tune that I don't like it. She's probably still practicing.

Father takes my hand and holds it very tight. "Keep perfectly calm," he says. At first I've no idea what's up, but then I see two policemen coming toward us. "Full of the joys of the chase?" Inge calls out to them. The policemen nod in a friendly way, because they can't understand what she said. One of them wags his finger at her—imagine breast-feeding a baby in public!

"But going around with loaded guns is just fine!" Inge calls after them. They don't turn around; they go on walking.

Father is white as a sheet.

"You look like a man with a guilty conscience," Inge says to Father. She has very sharp eyes.

"Well, I'm not," says Father, taking a deep breath. A little color comes back into his face. "I could do with a large cup of coffee now." He goes away again and comes back with cardboard cups of hot coffee, full to the brim. I drink a little of the strong coffee myself. It's too bitter for me, but it wakes me up.

Father says he'd love to take a bath now. What a funny thing to think of. I don't mind being dirty; it's much more fun. Perhaps I'll soon be so dirty no one will recognize me anymore. Then I won't have to wear clothes, because the layer of dirt will cover me all over from top to toe. And I'll always keep warm under it.

"No more bubble baths!" I shout. The sand in my hair does bother me a bit, but I can always shake that out. When I do, though, a grain of sand gets into baby Anna's eye and she starts crying. I'm sorry about that.

We pack our things in the black bag. That big white

48

boat, the ferry to Gomera, is still where it was last night. Father buys tickets. Inge and Anna and I sit on the sand, waiting. I draw little men in the sand with a stone.

"Has your vacation begun already?" asks Inge.

I shake my head.

"Do you live with your father?"

I don't say anything.

"Looking forward to Gomera?"

"Oh, leave me alone!" I hear myself telling Inge, and even as I say the words I'm feeling terribly sorry, because I didn't really want to say that sort of thing to her at all. I really wanted to tell her, for instance, that I think she's very, very nice, and Anna is sweet, and I like it when people talk to us.

"Sorry, sorry!" says Inge. "How was I to know you'd got out of your sleeping bag on the wrong side today!"

"It's okay," I mutter, wondering desperately what to do now. I jump up and kiss Inge on the cheek. Then I run off to stand in the line with Father. I look back at Inge. She blows me a kiss. It's nice that there's somebody who likes me.

KARL

It's good to know a few words of Spanish. When he has the ferry tickets in his hand, Karl feels the whole thing is highly improbable: the hot sun, when it's wintry, Christmas weather at home; the babble of foreign voices; Inge and her baby; the blue of the sea; the child skipping along beside him. Tina is the most improbable thing of all. She's so happy, exactly the way he wanted her to be. Karl is not quite sure why she isn't behaving differently: feeling sad, crying for her mother, being angry with him, fighting against being kidnapped, giving him up to the police. She is not doing any of that. Karl is annoyed with himself: Now he has everything he wanted, freedom and his child, and he still isn't happy. What, for heaven's sake, would make him happy? Perhaps time would change matters, if he went a long way away with Tina, to the other side of the Atlantic, or to Australia. Perhaps it's just a matter of getting used to things, and he would be really happy once he'd built his daughter a new nest. At the moment, however, he feels quite unable to do such a thing.

The first cars are being waved on into the ferry.

"Come on, we want to get a good place!" calls Inge. Tina lets go of Karl's hand and runs over to her. Inge has him thoroughly confused; he has never met anyone quite like her. It isn't that he has fallen in love with her or anything, but she is not what he thinks a woman should be. She seems to be so independent. Far more independent than he ever was. And she has such different goals in life. She doesn't care about being part of a proper family: father, mother, two children. Karl has always taken that kind of thing for granted. *Has* taken it for granted: exactly. Today, here and now, he is suddenly able to imagine quite different ways of life. Living as a hermit in the desert. As a grandfather in a huge peasant family. With a great many friends in a house in the country, surrounded by children and cows and nature.

What Karl cannot imagine any longer is living with Angelica in a little house on the outskirts of the city, seeing Tina and Tim only in the evenings, and getting older without anything exciting ever happening to him. Exactly what the exciting thing ought to be Karl does not yet know.

In any event, Karl Fechner is very, very confused. Nothing fits into place anymore.

They make their way up the steps into the boat. Inge clears them a path through the crowd by shouting, "Watch out—hot and sticky!" It is unlikely that many people understand what she is saying, but her tone of voice does the trick. Inge, baby Anna, and Tina disappear from sight behind a group of tall Canadian students.

Karl waves and calls, but the noise drowns out his voice. He battles with his rising panic: He mustn't lose Tina!

If Karl were not the sort of man who has been taught from early childhood that he must be strong, stronger, strongest, he would happily lean against the cool wall, slide down it to sit on the ground, and begin to cry. Or at least go to sleep.

However, Karl is Karl, so he suppresses his fear, but anyone who looked closely could see it in his eyes.

He is carried along by the crowd to the ship's refreshment stand, and decides to stay there and wait for the ferry to sail and the scurrying passengers to find seats. It seems like forever, and he has time to drink four cups of coffee before he can search for the others, his heart thumping. He finds baby Anna, Inge, and Tina sitting happily on a red leather bench quite close to a porthole.

"Oh, there you are!" says Tina. It sounds as if she didn't mind being parted from Karl at all.

Karl has never slapped his daughter, and he does not slap her now, but his hand itches to do it. He thinks she is too inconsiderate, scaring him like that and then acting as if it were nothing!

Everything is the wrong way around. Tina is in control of him, instead of Karl being in control of Tina. No, that wouldn't be right, either. Nobody ought to have control over another person.

A N G E L I C A

Tim snuggles up to Angelica, sucking his thumb. Angelica stares at the ceiling and thinks about her life so far.

Still no news of Tina. No phone call. No letter. Just silence, and it's only six days to Christmas.

"I haven't made Tina a present yet," says Tim, "but anyway, she isn't here, so I can make her something when she comes back."

Angelica does not reply.

Tim snuggles even closer to his mother. She is grateful for his affection. So young, and already such a comfort!

Then Tim goes out and comes back with Slow-and-Solid. "Slow-and-Solid's sad and lonely, too," he says, putting the tortoise on Angelica's pillow.

"Take her away!" cries Angelica. "Animals in bed—that's all we need!"

Sulking, Tim takes Slow-and-Solid off the pillow. Angelica shakes herself. She is not particularly fond of tortoises, though she rather likes turtle soup, but she would never have dared say so to Tim.

Tim's feelings are hurt.

"Daddy's mean," he says after a while, to please Angelica.

"No," says Angelica. "He's behaved very, very badly, but he is not mean."

"Bad and mean are the same thing," says Tim, going out on the balcony and perching Slow-and-Solid in a dangerous position on the balcony rail.

"It's not that simple," says Angelica, sitting up. "If it were that simple, then everything would be simple."

Tim giggles. "You're stupid!" he says, laughing, and rescues Slow-and-Solid just before she falls off the first-floor balcony. Angelica shakes her fist at Tim, and suddenly calls, "Tina, shut the door! There's a draft in here!"

She freezes, turns around once, and bursts into laughter. Tim tugs at her nightgown and asks, "Mommy, are you going really crazy now—are you, Mommy?"

Angelica picks Tim up, swings him around in the air, and hugs him. He can hardly breathe.

"Not to please you, my son!" says Angelica. Tim isn't quite sure whether she is laughing or crying until he sees the tears behind her laughter. Then he goes to his room, feeling sad.

He will never forget what Father did to her.

T I N A

What's the matter with Father? We've been out at sea for two hours, and he doesn't even look out the window, just keeps staring at his silly book. Once he was holding it upside down, and I had to turn it around for him. "San Sebastian, here we come," says Inge. She stands up and goes out on deck. I want to go with her, but Father calls me back.

"You stay here," he says, so I sit down again. "Come up on deck with us, Father," I say, trying to tempt him. "The sun's shining out there."

Father sighs and slowly puts his book away. I decide I don't particularly want to go on deck anymore. "We'll soon reach Gomera," I say, though, taking Father's hand and pulling him along.

The wind is strong, but lovely and salty. When I lick my lips they taste as if I'd been eating a bag of potato chips. My hair flies all over the place and keeps getting in my eyes. I know what: I'll cut it as short as Petra Auer's. Her hair's so short she looks like a hedgehog.

Father holds me when I climb up on the railing and spit into the water. Perhaps I'll spit on a shark, and it'll be so scared it will never come swimming close to land again. The little white town ahead of us is coming closer all the time. Gomera looks lovely. It has high mountains behind it—and the palm trees, lots of palm trees! I like palm trees. Because we don't have many of them back home, only parlor palms that are always wilting, at least ours do because nobody waters them, and Cactus sometimes pees on them when nobody's looking.

Father's hand is very cold when he helps me down again. "Are you feeling okay?" I ask. Father nods his head, but he doesn't look very well. We stay on deck until the last car has driven off the ferry. Finally a man who looks like the captain tells us to go ashore.

Inge's waiting, leaning on a post. Baby Anna is asleep again. She sleeps nearly all the time, and when she isn't asleep she's laughing or crying.

"I thought I'd wait for you—you look as if you don't know your way around."

Father nods gratefully. Inge leads us over to the buses. Oh, my goodness! All those people standing at the bus stop will never get into two buses!

"We'll have to wait," says Inge. I ask Father for money to buy a chocolate bar. It looks good but it tastes terrible. It's probably stale, because there are white specks in it. Father isn't looking, so I break off a piece and offer it to the big parrot hanging in a cage from the tree nearby.

"*Atención!*" shouts a man's voice behind me, and Father yanks my fingers away from the cage. The man is talking to us excitedly, and Inge nods. "He bites," she says.

"Last week he bit two fingers right off a little girl about your age."

I feel quite sick at the thought of it, Father looks angrily at me, and the parrot's owner waves his finger, but then gives me another horrible chocolate bar. I'll have to bury it somewhere, or maybe give it to somebody I don't like. No, that would be mean.

"Come to the Valley of Lone Mothers with us," says Inge. She's seen Father looking rather helplessly at the names on the buses. A third one has just come in: It says "Valle Gran Rey."

"Why lone mothers?" asks Father.

"I don't know why, either. There just are more and more mothers with children in Valle every year."

"Is it nice there?" Father asks Inge doubtfully.

Inge nods. "It would be fine for lone fathers, too," she says, and I tell her, "Father isn't alone, he's got me." I think Father is pleased to hear me say that.

Father turns pale during the bus ride. "I told you I can't ride at the back of a bus," he says. I really am worried about him now. We open a window; Father puts his head out, and then he feels better. I don't mind the way the bus sways. I wouldn't care how long the bus takes me around on the curves on this winding road— and the road is a very winding one.

Father tries not to look out anymore. He has a seat right by the window, and now the bus is going along the very edge of a cliff.

"Window seats aren't for sensitive people, not in these parts!" says Inge, laughing. "I know this road inside out, and I always sit in the middle of the bus!" She had told us earlier that this was a kind of anniversary for her: the tenth time she'd be going the same way. This was her fifth visit to Gomera. She tells us again.

"You ought to buy us a drink to celebrate," says a dark-skinned young man sitting in front of us.

Inge taps her forehead. "Somebody ought to buy *me* a drink to celebrate!" she says, and the young man offers her a bottle of wine, but Inge makes a face. "I'm not really into booze at this time of day," she says, and Father laughs because he thinks that sounds funny.

"Not into booze, eh?" He chuckles. "I'll have to bone up on young people's slang now that everything is going to be different!"

"So this is a turning point in your life?" asks Inge, interested. Father looks away. He says no more.

I stroke Anna. She has such a sweet little nose. I want to lick it, but I don't quite dare, because Inge might not like me to.

The baby laughs. She hasn't got any teeth at all; her mouth looks very funny, like Grandma Fechner's when she forgets to put her teeth back in, first thing in the morning.

Father's head is swaying from side to side. He doesn't look as pale as he did before; he's gone to sleep instead.

"He's nice, your father," says Inge.

I think so, too. "Only he's a bit difficult at times," I say, and I don't see why that makes some of the people sitting near us laugh all of a sudden.

"That is some cool baby!" says a man sitting in front

of me. I can't see much of him because of all his hair and his beard and his enormous eyebrows, but he has twinkling eyes.

"I'm not a baby," I tell him, and he says he's sorry and gives me a delicious pear.

I'm getting tired, too, and I'm hungry again. That disgusting chocolate bar won't go down, and just to make matters worse I realize I've been sitting on the second chocolate bar, the one the man gave me, and it's all over my pants, so they look as if I'd dirtied them. That looks really horrible.

Father wakes up when the bus is going around the last few bends in the road on its way down into the valley.

"Great!" he cries. "The most beautiful valley in the world!"

I've never seen any other valleys, but I think it's great, too. All those little houses, and the mules by the roadside, and the palm trees, and the women carrying heavy loads on their heads—I can't see how those huge pitchers don't crash to the ground. There must be a trick in it. Or else they have flat heads. This idea makes me laugh so much I choke.

"I stayed over there last year, in the house with the pink door—and two years ago I stayed in that one, the one with the big agave plant in front of it!" Inge's bouncing excitedly up and down in her seat, and baby Anna is getting bounced about, too, but she sleeps all the same. "That's where old Gonzalez lives, he sells *Papas con mojo*, that's potatoes with garlic sauce, and they're very cheap but you smell of garlic for weeks afterward," she says, "and over there is Tio Pepe's place, he'll be as toothless as ever and he looks quite terrifying, but he takes care of all the neighborhood babies. Jutta! Hi there, Jutta!" Inge has jumped up and is thumping the window right in front of Father's nose. Father pulls his head back in alarm. Inge shouts and waves through the bus window, but Jutta doesn't hear her. Jutta is out there in the road, a tall, blond woman, and, of course, she has a baby in a sling, too. She walks slowly on up the road, with two orange figures wearing medallions on their chests behind her, and a couple of skipping children with a birdcage behind them.

And then, at last, we see the sea ahead again. What waves! Waves as big as houses!

If they just have a few of my favorite comics here, I'll be happy to stay! Potatoes *con mojo* doesn't sound bad, either. We'll see what it's like in this place. . . .

K A R L

Karl and Tina and the black canvas bag are left behind at the bus stop on their own. Their fellow travelers have gone off into the little alleyways or toward the sea; they all seem to know where they're going. In fact they all have somewhere to go, except for Karl and Tina Fechner.

Inge and baby Anna have been swept away by a small group of people. Karl feels a little hurt.

"Now what?" asks Tina, patting her stomach, which promptly grumbles.

"I'm hungry, too!" Karl nods and takes Tina's hand. "But first we must find a place to stay."

However, that turns out to be difficult. What, now? At Christmastime? "Christmas," murmurs Karl. Tina has forgotten all about Christmas.

The innkeepers all throw their hands up in the air—not a room anywhere! They're as full as they can be, with beds crammed side by side in tiny little bedrooms.

The afternoon passes by, and Tina is getting worried. Her feet hurt, and she has had nothing to eat. The shops are closed and won't open again until five—not too long to wait. It's getting windy and it is uncomfortably chilly. Karl gets one of his own sweaters out of the black bag. Tina stupidly left her parka behind on the ferry. She looks funny in Karl's sweater, like a huge pullover on two legs, but it keeps her warm. She doesn't really mind what happens next if only she can get into a bed and close her eyes: Karl can tell that by the look on her face, and he feels guilty.

"Want to be carried!" says Tina, sounding like a toddler, and Karl does carry her until she gets too heavy for him.

"Listen, Tina, we'll give it one more try, shall we?" he says. If nothing comes of that, they will just have to spend the night on the beach, something Karl does not want to do at all. They only need a small room with a door to shut behind them, a room where they can catch their breath and think things over.

To make matters worse, it looks like rain—and it hardly

ever rains here! But sure enough, heavy raindrops are beginning to fall on the sandy path, turning it into mud. They stand in a doorway and wait for the shower to stop; it passes over as suddenly as it came.

Karl is feeling furious with himself. Just like you, he thinks: First you kidnap your daughter, then you can't even provide her with a roof over her head! Your rotten luck, Karl Fechner! "My rotten luck!" he says out loud, and at least that makes the sullen Tina smile again.

They are standing outside a tall, gray building, with a sign saying *APARTAMIENTOS*. When Karl, who has been carrying Tina again, puts her down on the steps he does not feel very hopeful. Tina immediately slumps down on top of the black canvas bag like a deflated balloon.

But this time Karl's luck has changed. What the small, fat owner of the place offers him is not an *apartamiento*, but at least it is a room—a very strange-looking room.

It is enormous and divided up by long rows of shelves. Right at the back there is a small, empty corner, and right beside that a washroom with a toilet. Some steps lead up to a glazed-in cubbyhole by the wall on the right.

"What is it?" Karl asks the fat little man in Spanish, and Señor Feliz explains proudly that they are in a supermarket, which is due to open in four weeks' time.

"I see," says Karl. Señor Feliz tells Karl and Tina to wait, and a little later he comes back through the rolled-up shutters, panting under the weight of two folded cots, which he puts down in the little corner by the washroom. Karl soon works out the complicated mechanism of the beds, and Tina drops on one without a word. She looks angry. Karl glances at her doubtfully, and then Señor Feliz reappears for the second time, carrying pillows and blankets. He shows Karl how to open and close the shutters, takes a week's payment in advance, and goes away. Tina looks around her; she feels scared. Footsteps echo in the tall room, and when you say something there is a little echo, too. She explores the rows of shelves, and when she finds the steps up to the glazed cubbyhole she runs up them, feeling cheerful once more. She gets behind the glass and calls down, "Got you, Karl Fechner! You kidnapped your daughter!"

Karl hardly knows whether to laugh or cry, but he laughs when he sees Tina looking happy again.

There is a loud knock on the shutters. It is Señor Feliz again, carrying two bottles of fruit juice and two more of the rancid chocolate bars. Tina makes a face, but not so that Señor Feliz can see her.

When at last he goes away, she leaps over the beds, flings her arms around Karl, and cries, "We've got a supermarket of our very own!" Then Karl and Tina Fechner dance exuberantly around the room, until they realize that it has gotten dark outside, but the light is on in here, and there are several people standing outside the big plate-glass window with their noses pressed to it, laughing their heads off.

Karl closes the second shutter, and they lie down on their beds and sleep for an hour and twenty-five minutes; it is exactly that length of time before Señor Feliz bangs on the metal shutters, wanting the empty fruit juice bottles back. Feeling extraordinarily well and happy, Karl and his daughter get off the beds and decide to explore Valle Gran Rey and have a really good meal, whatever it costs.

And for the first time since the beginning of their adventurous journey Karl feels, as he puts it to himself, happy as a lark.

ANGELICA

The telephone rings, and Angelica leaps toward it. She must have set a world record in running to answer the phone these last few days, not that she has ever gotten any reward for her pains.

When she hears the words, "This is Police Station Five," she holds her breath and feels that her heart is racing. I can't stand it, I shall fall down dead, she thinks; but then, all of a sudden, her heart is beating normally and she can breathe again.

There is no news. The police have called only to find out if Angelica has heard where her daughter is.

No. She has not.

"Just asking out of personal interest," says the policeman, clearing his throat.

Without a word, Angelica hangs up, and is immediately sorry. Perhaps he really did mean well. But there was nothing else she could do. She has been home from work the last two days, pleading illness. And this is Christmastime, too, with only four days to go, when more books are taken out of the library than usual. The children stock up on reading matter for the Christmas vacation, in case they aren't given enough books as presents, or the books they do get are boring. So Karin, the other librarian, is left on her own to deal with a crowd of impatient children all wanting to borrow the same books. Books about horses, horses, and more horses . . . Angelica can't stand horse books, but the children seem to love them. Angelica hopes that Karin does not mind. She may even believe Angelica is sick, since although she does not really know why, Angelica has not told her a word about the kidnapping of Tina. That may be because if she did, it would make it seem so much more real. Everyone would say sympathetic things to her, or start bad-mouthing Karl.

Thank goodness my mother doesn't know, thinks Angelica. She would be sure to say, "I told you that man was no good fifteen years ago." And although Angelica's mother always acted as if she really liked Karl, right now she'd regard him as a stranger. . . . Angelica catches herself silently defending Karl to her mother.

"Who cares what anyone else thinks?" Angelica cries out to her reflection in the mirror. It is not a very attractive reflection. She has dark rings under her eyes, she is pale, her hair is messy, and her shoulders sag.

"I've a perfect right to look the way I feel," Angelica tells her reflection.

Tim is still at school; it is the last day of the term. She is glad he's out. She needs time to recover. It is not that she can't concentrate on the books she is trying to read. It is not that she can't manage to knit the sleeve of Tim's Christmas sweater without dropping stitches all the time. But whatever she does, she is all worked up inside.

How nice to be perfectly calm.

It's awful to be so helpless. In fact, that is the very worst thing about it: feeling that there is nothing, nothing at all she can do except sit there waiting and waiting until she hears from Tina and Karl again.

"I wish I knew what's going on in Karl's mind," mutters Angelica. Is he enjoying himself with Tina? Does he think about Angelica's troubles? She has no idea. For years, Angelica thought she knew Karl inside out: all his good points and his bad points. And now she realizes she knows nothing at all about him. She never believed it was more than a casual remark when he said he could never give up Tina. Incredible to think he'd actually kidnapped his child.

Angelica prowls restlessly around the house. "Oh, do stop it!" she shouts at Cactus, who is trotting along after her, turning whenever she does. Cactus gets on her nerves. Sometimes she stops outside Tina's door, puts her hand on the doorknob, and then walks on. She cannot simply walk into the room, because she has locked it and put the key high up at the back of a closet. She doesn't want to go into Tina's room; she knows very well that if she does she will cry all day. Angelica turns on the television—at ten in the morning! A newscaster. A newscaster with a boring face; she can't stand it! Angelica turns it off again, fast, and wishes she had an on-off button to turn off her misery; to turn on happiness.

She goes back to the mirror and paints around her eyes with a black felt pen. Then she paints a big black button on her nose, and presses it. Of course nothing happens, not even when she tries again.

Someone rings the doorbell. Angelica goes to open it. The mailman looks at her in surprise. "Carnival makeup at Christmastime?" he asks, handing Angelica a letter, a pencil, and a piece of paper.

No, it is not from Tina and Karl. The address is in Grandma Fechner's writing, and yet again Grandma Fechner has not put the proper stamps on. Angelica signs for the letter and pays the excess postage.

"Thanks," says the postman, and adds, "Er . . . you've got something on your nose, Mrs. Fechner."

"That is my on-off button," says Angelica gravely.

"Of course," says the postman. "Well, Merry Christmas." He touches his hat and goes off shaking his head but grinning.

Angelica wipes her nose and opens Grandma Fechner's letter with her black fingers. It contains seasonal good wishes to the dear children, and a check for Christmas presents. Sighing, Angelica puts the letter behind the mirror. She will have to answer it very soon.

"Don't want to," she tells the mirror, giving it a shove. She holds her breath. The letter falls down, but the mirror stays put.

Perhaps that is a good sign.

TINA

I still can't believe how warm it is here. I put on a thick sweater over my T-shirt as usual this morning, and what happens? I sweat like a pig! It was really great yesterday evening. We were so hungry we just followed the smell of garlic and ended up in a little restaurant where you could get lots of delicious fish, very cheap. The restaurant was full of people, and there were a great many children there, too, little ones, and bigger ones about ten years old, almost like me. We met a French-woman with a little boy named Pierre, who looks like Tim. Then all of us children went out, though it was pitch dark, and we found stones on the beach, huge stones but not too heavy, and we built castles and caves with them. Pierre and I collected most of the stones. There was one rather stupid girl there, a German girl, who just sat and shouted orders and thought she was too good to join in. I can't stand that sort of person.

And there were two Spanish boys, and a girl from England, and a few more children who spoke German. It didn't bother us that we spoke different languages; we all knew just what the others meant, though I'm not sure how.

I didn't go to bed till two in the morning! Mother would have been furious if she'd known, but it was great fun. Father stayed in the restaurant while I was playing, and he wasn't bored at all. Actually I think he had a bit too much to drink. Whenever I looked in the restaurant he was smiling happily, nodding his head, and the bottle in front of him was getting emptier.

He talked a lot to the Frenchwoman, who spoke good German, and two English people who were sitting at his table, too. I never knew Father could speak English so well—at least, the English people kept laughing when Father said something. He sounded so cheerful I think he was telling them jokes.

Now it's eleven in the morning. It was odd, waking up in the middle of all these shelves. Father was lying on his back with his mouth open, snoring. He didn't wake up until just now, when I was already dressed and kneeling beside him to see how many fillings he has in his teeth. Then he suddenly closed his mouth and opened his eyes.

"Don't look a gift horse in the mouth," he muttered, closing his eyes, opening them again, closing them again—and then he shook himself and sat up, and he and the cot toppled over.

He looks so funny sitting there on the floor, frowning, and needing a shave, with the bed behind his head!

"And what would you like today, sir?" I ask. "How about our special offer, a delicious glass of water, half price for you?" I go into the tiny bathroom and get him some water.

"Thanks, that's a real bargain," he says, and drinks it all up. "More, please." He hands me back the glass. Father drinks four glasses of water, just like a thirsty horse.

"Drank a bit too much yesterday," says Father, shaking himself. "Never again! Well, good morning, little one!" He kisses me on the end of my nose, and suddenly I feel I really love him a lot, and I jump up at him, and then we both topple over backwards.

Father puts on clean clothes and stuffs our dirty things into a bag. He taps his wallet. "All our money's in here, Tina," he says, and he thinks for a moment. "Perhaps I shouldn't keep it all together? It would be risky to leave it here. . . ." He taps his wallet again. "No, you'd better stay in there," he says to the money and his passport, which is in there, too.

We go out to get some breakfast. There are terraces covered with straw right by the beach, with tables on them. There are such big waves again that they cover the whole village with a light mist as they break. I can feel the moisture on the tip of my nose. I've gotten used to tasting like salt now.

It's noisy. The sea can make a lot of noise, especially when the beach isn't sandy but it's big stones instead, being rolled around by the waves. They'll be sand, too, in a few thousand years, right?

Father comes back to me with two rolls even bigger than the ones we had on the dock. I can't decide which side to start eating—my mouth's too small to bite right through my roll.

Father realizes I'm baffled. He takes the roll back from me again, takes it apart, and covers each half with a slice of cheese. "There you are, love, it's easier now!" We laugh. Sometimes I'm rather dense, and I think for ages when the solution's really quite simple! I'm much smarter when it comes to complicated things, honestly I am!

"Pierre!" I shout. It's as if the little boy had spent all night collecting stones, because there he is at it again. I run down to him, and he grins.

"Tina!" he says in his funny French accent, and he

says something else in French, too. I don't understand the words, but I can tell he wants me to play with him. I run back to Father, take a mouthful of hot milk, choke on it, and run off, calling back, "I'm busy, Father!"

Father stays on the terrace, looking out to sea. Talk about lazy! Building stone castles is much more fun.

K A R L

Karl watches sadly as his daughter runs busily back and forth, carrying stones. Soon she is surrounded by other children, laughing happily with them. He can't remember whether he used to make friends so easily himself, as a child. But he finds it difficult now that he is grown-up. Grown-up? Karl does not feel at all grown-up. He does not want to be grown-up, if it means knowing everything, seeing your way clear ahead, taking responsibility the whole time. Adults may not fool around. Karl likes to fool around. Adults may not be unsure of themselves. Karl is unsure of himself. Adults may not cry into their pillows at night. But Karl sometimes does.

Who says what adults must be like?

Karl gets a fourth cup of coffee from the restaurant, which is slowly filling up. This place is full of late risers.

"You look very thoughtful again!" There is Inge all of a sudden, standing beside Karl and smiling all over her cheerful face. Anna is peering out of her sling at the world, a little grumpily. Perhaps she didn't have a good night's sleep.

"Oh, I'm fine!" Karl tries to look relaxed and laugh.

Inge points to the beach. "Tina feels at home already, I can see!"

Karl nearly says she feels better here than she does at home, but instead he says, "It's easy for her," and at the same moment he thinks, Wait, that's not true, in fact it is far from easy for her, being here with me.

"Yes?" says Inge, rather doubtfully, shaking her head. She narrows her eyes and points her finger at the third button down on Karl's shirt. She is a head shorter than Karl.

"There's something wrong with you two."

Karl pulls in his stomach and holds his breath.

"I bet your buttock muscles are all tensed up, too," says Inge.

Karl lets his breath out sharply through his teeth. What nerve! But when he thinks about it he discovers that she's right; he *is* tensing his buttock muscles.

"You're tense all over," says Inge, grasping the muscles at the nape of Karl's neck. "There!"

She presses quite hard, and Karl lets out a yelp, seeing stars.

"Where did you learn that?" he asks, with a wry smile. Just a little bit of pressure, and it hurt so much.

"I'm a masseuse," says Inge. "I spend all day working with tense people. Don't worry, you're not the only one."

"Sometimes you do get to feel you're alone in the world, though," mutters Karl, sipping his coffee.

Inge picks up her glass of orange juice from the counter.

"Listen, if you're in trouble, we're around most of the time." Then she leaves. Karl stands there, at a loss, and feels someone push him. "Out of the way." A young man shoves Karl to the right; he does not resist. "Do you mind?" the young man asks a little more politely, but he is determined to get in first; he is addressing a red-haired young woman and reaching for the coffee the man behind the counter is pushing her way. Karl feels someone push him to the left. He leaves the restaurant, walking backwards, and goes back to the terrace. His shoulders are sagging.

Tina is still playing on the beach. Karl begins counting waves.

"Come along," Inge says behind him. Karl obediently stands up and follows her to a spot on the beach where there is a heap of dry seaweed. "Take your shirt off and lie down," says Inge. Karl is not sure what is going on, but he does as he is told. "On your stomach," says Inge. She takes off the sling and lays Anna down between two stones that will give her shade. Inge kneels over Karl.

"Close your eyes," she says. She takes a jar of cream out of her shoulder bag, rubs her hands with it, and begins to massage Karl's back.

It hurts so much that Karl clenches his teeth.

"You'll soon feel relaxed, really relaxed," says Inge, running her hands all the way down a long muscle. The pain is going away, and now it is pleasant. "There's so much that comes out, once your muscles are relaxed. That's where all your fears gather into little lumps." Inge goes on massaging him for a long time. Karl does not know how long; he has lost his sense of time. But at some point, in the middle of it, he begins to cry. He cries quietly into the seaweed.

For the first time ever, he does not mind someone seeing him cry.

T I N A

This is a lovely day! It's hot, and I'm not wearing anything except the little bathing suit we bought me in the shop over there. I'm glad I don't have sensitive skin! I never turn red, I tan right away. I think I look wonderful, like a roast chicken. I hope nobody eats me up.

I'd better take a look at Father. He's probably still sitting up there drinking cup after cup of coffee. No, the table's empty. But I can see Inge.

"Your father's asleep down on the beach," she says. "Be nice to him, he's in a bad way."

Asleep! How can Father sleep now, when the sun's shining and the waves are getting bigger all the time, and there are so many things to see? And what does she mean, he's in a bad way? Because he drank so much yesterday, or what?

I run down to the place Inge pointed out. Father is lying there with his shirt over his head. His back is all red. He'll get terribly sunburned if he doesn't get up right away.

"Wake up, Father! Come in the water with me!" I call. "We can jump the waves now!"

Father looks at me in a very funny way. Oh, all right, then. I run into the breakers, splash about there, and then run back to Father. I act like Cactus, shaking myself, and Father splutters. It's so hot that the drops of water off me almost hiss when they fall on his skin.

"Oh, Tina," sighs Father, and then I sit beside him and put my head on his shoulder. "Now shall we go and jump the waves?" he asks after a while.

I nod. Father takes his trousers off; he's wearing trunks underneath. We run into the water hand in hand, singing.

The cold Atlantic Ocean wakes Father right up. He dives down under and through a wave. Well, I can do that, too! I'm a good swimmer. We're two fish.

"You'll grow fins yet!" shouts Father. An enormous wave comes rolling up and knocks him over. I try to help him up, but the next wave is already on its way. We can hardly get our breath back. The Atlantic is a nasty, treacherous ocean! Father stands up again, holds out his arms, and I run into them.

Father holds me tight. He says something, but so quietly I can't hear it.

"What?" I shout before the next wave breaks.

"You look like Angelica," says Father, and his eyes are wet, whether with water or tears I don't know. I'm afraid it's tears.

"Silly!" I shout, and I run away and set off to swim to America.

ANGELICA

Angelica opens the door. Rainer is standing outside: Rainer, who sits next to Tina at school. He shifts his weight from one leg to the other, looking embarrassed. "I only wanted to ask ... er ..." he stammers. "About Tina ... is she back yet?"

Angelica shakes her head and presses her lips together. Rainer takes his hand from behind his back and holds a package out to Angelica.

"It's for Tina ... when she comes back, okay?" Rainer turns and runs off down the garden path.

Angelica stands there in the doorway with the package in her hand for a long time. Then, slowly, she goes upstairs to Tina's room. Cactus follows her, snuffling sadly. Angelica stands on tiptoe and gets the key out of the closet. She unlocks the door. Without looking to right or to left, she goes up to Tina's desk. There is an open notebook on the desk, and a fountain pen with its top off. Angelica puts the package down on the book, picks up the fountain pen, puts the top on, takes it off again, puts the pen back exactly the way she found it, and leaves Tina's room. She locks the door, puts the key back in the closet, and goes down to the living room with Cactus still at her heels. As if he did not want to let Angelica out of his sight.

The calendar in the kitchen says it is the twenty-second of December. Three days to go until Christmas. There is sleet falling outside. A Christmas tree, which is now getting wet, is leaning against the garden gate waiting to be brought in.

"It's all right, it's all right!" A black-and-white dog with floppy ears and legs like a dachshund, but three times a dachshund's size, is barking at me.

"Woof, woof, woof, woof!"

When the dog realizes I'm not going to hurt him— I'm just standing quietly in front of him—he barks once more and then comes closer. He even lets me pat his head.

"Your name is Woof!" I tell him.

"Woof, woof, woof!" barks Woof, but not nearly as loud as before, and he is wagging his tail, too. He jumps up at me and licks my face. "Yuk! Don't do that, Woof!" I walk on a little way and then look around. Woof pricks up his ears and starts moving, too, but he keeps a couple of yards behind me. When I move on, so does Woof. If I stop, Woof sits down and waits.

I'm glad to have a dog again. "Come on, Woof!" I call, and sure enough, Woof is right behind me now, then beside me, jumping up at me. He runs ahead for a little way, comes back to make sure I'm still here, and I can see he's glad, too. We run along the beach. Woof hops over the big stones like a rabbit. He gets his paws wet and shakes himself.

"Hello!" We've come to a sudden halt in front of Father, who is sitting on our sleeping bag reading. He is wearing a paper bag on his head to keep the sun off.

"This is Woof," I tell him.

Father looks at Woof in surprise. "What an extraordinary mixture!" he says. "At least five breeds of dog went into his making!" But I can see he likes Woof. Woof lies down beside Father.

"Do you know what day it is?" asks Father. I shake my head. What day? I've no idea. I haven't been keeping count of the days since we got here. All I know is that when I go to sleep every night in our supermarket bedroom, I'm already looking forward to the next day, and the beach, and playing with the other children.

"Christmas Eve," says Father.

I have to sit down and think about that. He must be right. I count on my fingers. We left home over a week ago. Ages ago, though the time seems to have gone so quickly.

I look up at the sky. Christmas Eve? The sky is bright blue and the sun is beating down on us. There are people wearing bathing suits and bikinis, and toddlers with nothing on at all, and ice cream cones, and suntan lotions, and sunburned noses and red shoulders. It's not at all like my idea of Christmas. Christmas should be the way it is in Christmas stories, with cold weather outside, and snow on the ground, and there should be a big Christmas tree with Grandma Fechner's old Christmas decorations on it, and the smell of the special cake Grandma bakes, and Tim with a stomachache from eating the uncooked dough left in the mixing bowl, and Mother and Father stuffing the goose together, and a bell ringing to say it's time to open our presents, and . . .

"What are you thinking about?" Father gently touches my shoulder.

Woof is trotting up and down the beach. Don't run away, Woof. Mother will be walking down the road with

Cactus now. Tim will be whizzing along the sidewalk on his bike in spite of the snow, getting dangerously close to the curb and forgetting to watch out for the gates to people's driveways.

No, it won't be like that after all. Everything will be different from usual today, because it's Christmas. And I'm not at home. Mother will be crying, the way I'm crying now. Cactus's ears will be drooping. Slow-and-Solid will crawl away and hide.

We spent last Christmas all together.

Almost like a proper family.

Father is rocking me in his arms. "Listen, shall we go and look for a Christmas tree?" he asks. I nod and swallow.

"Come on, Woof!" Woof really does answer to his name; he comes with us. We go up the road to the village, past the banana plantations. The bananas aren't ripe yet; they hang from the trees in hard green bunches.

We meet several people we know from talking to them in the restaurant or on the beach. It's funny the way most of them only say hello and nothing else, even when Father spent a lot of time talking to them the evening before. Almost as if they forget you very quickly. We haven't seen Inge for a couple of days, either. I wonder where she and her baby are?

A black-haired woman with no teeth, carrying a pitcher on her head, comes toward us. She's very old, but she doesn't have a single white hair. She knows me; she's always kind to us children. Usually she has a few dates in her apron pocket to give us.

"Did you know it's Christmas Eve today?" Yvonne

comes skipping down the road, with her parents after her. I played a game about Sleeping Beauty with Yvonne for two whole days.

I nod. Yvonne skips on, and her parents say hello. Father says hello, too, and that's all the conversation we have.

"They don't like us," says Father. He sounds depressed.

"That's not true!" I say. I'm sure they like us. But Father looks so sad all the time I expect people are afraid his sadness might be catching. It can be catching, too.

We cross a banana plantation and the bed of a dried-up stream. It seems to me that Father knows where he's going.

"Where are we going?" I ask. He looks mysterious. "I've seen something we could use as a Christmas tree," he says.

Then I see it, too. There's a little group of cacti; that's what he means.

How are we going to get one of those prickly cacti out of the ground, though? Father takes his beautiful Swiss knife out of his pocket and saws away at a cactus. It's hard work. "Tough as rubber!" grunts Father. White, sticky, milky stuff comes out of the cactus. Beads of perspiration on his forehead, Father cuts through it. "There!" he says, triumphantly holding our Christmas tree up. A splash of cactus juice lands on his nose and another on Woof's muzzle. Woof jumps up and rubs his muzzle with his paw. The stuff is sticky.

We go back to our supermarket with the dripping

cactus. So now I know why Father brought a hollow brick along yesterday evening: The cactus fits nicely into it. Our Christmas-tree cactus looks funny standing in the middle of the room.

"We need candles," says Father. Still followed by Woof, we go up to the village again and into a small shop. You could easily pass its tiny, crooked door if you didn't know there was a shop on the other side, a shop selling just about everything people need to live here, which isn't all that much. I don't think there are any huge stores in these parts, like the shops at home.

One thing they don't need here is Christmas-tree candles. There aren't any in the shop. So we buy a bit of wire and some ordinary big candles. Father has another good idea, but he isn't telling me what it is yet. However, he buys a package of spaghetti.

Back home—and I can't help laughing to find myself calling the supermarket home—we make candleholders out of the wire and put the big candles in them. It's very hard attaching the candles to the Christmas-tree cactus. You have to use a lot of force to wind the wire around the branches of the cactus, and if it cuts in too much, the milky cactus juice oozes out and drips on the tiled floor.

And then, of course, the cactus juice sticks to my sneakers, and I leave white footprints all over the room and even out in the street, because you can't wash the cactus juice off with water. Father gets rid of it later with lighter fluid.

"What's the spaghetti for?" I ask. "We're not going to eat it raw, are we? Without any sauce, either? Yuk!"

I make a face, but Father goes out into the street, looking mysterious again, and soon comes back with a pan and a small gas burner.

"I've only borrowed it," he says. He puts water on to boil and cooks the spaghetti.

"What about the sauce?" I grumble, because the sight of spaghetti always makes me hungry.

"We don't need sauce," says Father.

He drains the spaghetti, pours some cold water over it, and then fishes it out of the pan with his hands. He lets it drip over the sink.

"Did you wash your hands?" I ask, because Father's always asking me if I've washed my hands, but he often forgets himself. Guiltily, Father shakes his head. "But it doesn't matter," he explains. He goes over to the cactus and hangs the spaghetti on it, neatly draping a couple of white tubes over each branch. "Christmas-tree decorations," says Father.

I fall on the floor laughing, and Woof leaps excitedly around me. He probably thinks I've gone crazy.

"Oh, Father, that's really great!" I gasp.

KARL

Christmas. Karl has never felt so un-Christmassy on December twenty-fourth as he does today. He keeps hoping Tina won't notice how hard he is working to control himself. He is pretending to be cheerful. Karl Fechner, the man nothing ever bothers! The friend and father who'll do anything to make his daughter happy!

While all the time he is feeling miserable—so miserable he can't think of any suitable comparison for it.

He does not want a cactus for a Christmas tree. He wants to be at home beside a real tree with Angelica, maybe even holding hands with her, and he wants Tina and Tim to be there. Now that Tina is here with him, he realizes for the first time how much he loves Tim, too.

Karl wants everything to be the way it used to be. Perhaps it wasn't so bad after all.

What a lot of trouble Christmas is giving me, thinks Karl. Christmas, the time for families to be together.

ANGELICA

At the very same moment, Angelica is standing by the window. It is snowing. Real Christmas weather, just like it ought to be.

Tim is still out at his friend Pip's, but the bell will ring any minute now and he will come in.

There is a tall Christmas tree in the middle of the room, plain green and without any decorations yet.

They used to decorate the Christmas tree together. Angelica and Karl.

82

Angelica cannot do it alone today; she would rather have Tim help her.

She has no idea how she is going to get through the evening. She will try hard to make it a happy Christmas for Tim. Angelica rubs furiously at the misted window-pane. Maternal thoughts in her head again! Thinking what her child will like all the time, putting him first. But what about me, thinks Angelica, who's going to make it a happy Christmas for me?

How she would love to have Tina in her arms now! Her dearest wish is for the door to open and for Tina to come in, with Karl behind her—and for none of it to have happened at all. No quarrels, no divorce, no kid-napping.

Oh, stop feeling so sorry for yourself, Angelica, she thinks, and goes to the door. Tim is home.

T I N A

It won't be a real Christmas. The people of Gomera celebrate the birth of Christ on December twenty-fifth, the same as us, but they don't give presents until Twelfth Night.

Will I get anything? I'm not sure. With everything so different from usual, maybe there won't be any presents.

Father says we must wait to light the candles until it's dark, or it won't be like Christmas.

There's no smell of baking.

No smell of Christmas dinner.

Is Mother having the same sort of Christmas as usual? With Tim and Cactus and Slow-and-Solid?

I pat Woof, and he growls contentedly. He's all right.

Perhaps Mother doesn't mind that I'm not at home.

"I bet Mother's glad I've gone away. It's less trouble for her," I say. I'm sitting on the cot staring at the Christmas-tree cactus. Father has rolled up the shutters and put our only chair in the sun. He's taking a nap—not a real one; he's just dozing off.

"What was that you said?" Father wakes up with a start.

"Mother must be glad I've gone away," I repeat. Father begins to bite his lip. "Listen, Tina . . ." he says, and then he can't go on.

"One child is less work than two," I say, shrugging my shoulders, "and if she really wanted to find me she would have found me by now."

Then I keep quiet, perfectly quiet, because Father is looking angrily at me—so angrily I feel a cold shiver run down my spine.

"Don't you ever say that again," he says slowly.

"N-no, Father," I say. I don't really know why I'm talking such nonsense today.

Yes, I do know.

I want to go back to Mother. I want to go home.

I try persuading my homesickness to go away, but it's no good. It won't go. It's taken root under that Christmas-tree cactus.

Father's chair isn't in the sun anymore. Or rather, the

sun isn't shining on Father's chair, because the chair itself is still in the same place. Well, anyway, it's beginning to get dark outside; it's getting dark faster and faster.

Father stands up and looks for his matches. "Now we'll light the candles," he says. His voice sounds hollow, because the walls of this place are all bare except for the empty shelves.

He strikes a match and then blows it out again. "I forgot something," he says, and blows his nose. He goes over to the black canvas bag and takes a tiny package out of it. It is wrapped in Christmas paper.

"A present for you," says Father, putting it down on the hollow brick that holds the Christmas-tree cactus in position. Then he lights the candles, and I realize, with an awful sinking feeling, that I don't have a present for him. I never even thought of it. How horrible of me.

I'm so horrible it makes me feel quite sick.

The candles flicker.

It is a bit like Christmas after all. Only the smell of scorched spaghetti isn't at all Christmassy.

I unwrap my present.

Oh, great! A Swiss knife just like Father's! I've wanted one for ages, because with a knife like that nothing could happen to me if I ever got lost. It has two blades, a pair of scissors, a pair of pincers, a toothpick, a nail file, and a bottle opener.

"Thank you, Father." I give Father a Christmas kiss, and then I stick my knife into the cactus until a candle falls off and goes out.

"Oh, God," says Father, sitting down on the chair again. It's quite chilly now. Father buries his face in his hands and begins to cry. I have to listen hard to make out that as well as crying, he's trying to sing "Silent Night."

That makes me cry, too. I sit at Father's feet and we both cry together. Feeling sad hurts so much.

"Well, Christmas is *almost* spelled Cry-stmas," I say, when at last I've run out of tears.

Father puts his arms around me, hugs me tight, and just says, "Yes, Tina."

But it was a lousy joke.

KARL

So there it is, just the way he didn't want it: the most miserable Christmas of his life, a mediocre present for Tina, and tears on top of it.

Karl Fechner has had enough. Things can't go on like this. His time with Tina is too precious to be wasted in tears. Karl pulls himself together and tries to look cheerful. He begins eating the spaghetti off the tree. It doesn't taste good cold.

"Well, now we'll give ourselves a really good Christmas dinner, Tina!" says Karl. "Come along, let's dress up!" He changes his trousers and sweater, and Tina brushes her hair until it shines and feels really good to touch.

They walk along the beach. Woof frisks about, running ahead of them and looking forward to a Christmas steak or, at least, a Christmas sausage.

Far off, where the sand dunes start, they see people around a fire.

"There's Inge!" cries Tina, running to her. Yes, it is Inge. Anna is lying on a blanket with two other babies, all of them asleep. Tina thinks they look sweet, like baby dolls.

"Where've you been?" asks Tina.

Inge points to the mountains at the end of the valley. "Over there," she says. "It was marvelous."

Karl comes slowly walking up, too. He always approaches groups of people with great caution.

"You don't look any better yet," says Inge. Karl thinks this is rude of her, but he can't really take offense; she probably just sees it as honesty. What's more, she is probably right. It is a long time since he took a good look at himself in a mirror; he avoids mirrors if possible.

"Merry Christmas!" calls a cheerful young man.

"Thanks," says Karl gloomily. He does not feel like being part of a merry crowd; he wants to be alone with Tina, eating dinner with her, and forgetting that awful present-giving session over their cold spaghetti.

"Sit down," Inge tells them.

Tina would like to stay here, but Karl says quickly, "No, thanks, we're on our way to dinner." He glances at a large stone where a quantity of chops, steaks, and sausages are lying. There are potatoes, bananas, and apples as well.

"We're about to cook all that—there'll be enough for you, too," Inge tempts them yet again.

"Oh, please, Father," says Tina.

Karl can't say yes. He would like to grant Tina her wish, but he simply could not stand being with these good-humored people. He would be sure to spoil their evening.

"Let him be, he doesn't want to be with us," says a young woman. Tina has seen her with Inge before.

Gently but firmly, Karl pulls Tina away. The decision is a hard one for Woof, too: Must he really leave a place where there'd be delicious things like chop bones? Should he go with his new owners?

"Come on, Woof!" Tina calls, sparing him the agony of choosing. He turns away sadly, looking back once or twice as the chops and sausages dwindle in the distance.

Tina's sneakers are full of sand. She looks gloomily at the ground. It's not fair of Karl, simply dragging her away from a place where everyone's so happy. As if he were afraid of happiness.

There's still room for them in El Cid. Tina is angry at her father, so angry she says she isn't hungry. She does not give up her hunger strike until Karl orders several delicious things.

She still wants to annoy him, though. She orders three apple dumplings with sugar and cinnamon, all for her.

"Typical Canary Islands dish!" says Karl, and they both laugh, because, of course, the apple dumplings are more German than anything else; a lot of German tourists come here, and the owners want to serve what will sell well.

Anyway, the owner of El Cid serves Tina her apple dumplings, each on its own plate, and the dumplings are so big hanging over the rims. Tina is full after the first dumpling. She surreptitiously slips a handful of apple dumpling under the table. Woof tactlessly snuffles at it so loudly that Karl looks under the table, but he pretends he didn't see anything. Tina breathes a sigh of relief. Woof is disappointed. He doesn't like sweet things. Tina wipes her greasy fingers on the tablecloth, and Woof growls. "Sneak!" hisses Tina. Karl has eaten well: a plateful of delicious shrimp and garlic sauce. He orders coffee. Then he lays his hand on Tina's.

"Tina, would you like to start a new life with me in South America?"

Tina sits there, rigid.

"I'm sure I could soon find work there; I've been thinking it over carefully these last few days. There'd be sure to be an opening for me as a farm manager. You'd soon learn the language, and you could go to school there. I know somebody in Brazil, and—"

"No!" cries Tina, jumping up. She begins to cry.

"I want to go home! I want to go home *now*!" she shouts.

Horrified, Karl looks around him and whispers, "All right, all right!" Nervously, he gulps his coffee. He has broken out in a sweat. He hadn't expected Tina to take it like that.

"It was only a joke, Tina, only a joke," he adds quickly. Tina calms down again.

"Really?" She glances up at him.

Karl nods and tries to smile. "Really!"

Tina has a huge dish of ice cream. She is beginning to feel sick, what with all the apple dumplings and now the cold ice cream on top of them, and the three little bottles of pear juice she drank, too.

Karl asks for the bill. The waiter writes it all out, tears the piece of paper off his pad, and lets it fall on the table in front of Karl. Tina tries to read the amount upside down, but she can't.

"What's the matter, Father?"

Karl is sitting there as if thunderstruck. His right hand is resting on his breast pocket, and he is staring past Tina, muttering something she cannot make out. Then he stands up and begins frantically searching his pockets. Tina can't help laughing. "You look as if you're trying to catch a flea!" She giggles.

"My wallet's gone!" croaks Karl.

"What?" Tina looks surprised. At first she doesn't understand; then she does. "Really gone? With your passport and all?"

Karl sits down and nods mechanically.

"That means we've had dinner and can't pay for it?" asks Tina.

The young woman at the next table, who knows them by sight, leans over. "Can I help out?"

Karl says nothing, and Tina answers, "That would be great!"

Then Karl whispers, "Yes, if you would!" He is in a state of great confusion. The waiter is surprised to see the young woman take out her purse and pay the bill.

"You'll pay me back tomorrow, okay?" she says, giving them both a friendly nod.

"Good-bye," Karl says in a hollow voice, and then shakes himself and says, "Thank you!" to her as she leaves.

"Well, it's all over now, Tina," says Karl dejectedly. "We haven't any money left at all, no traveler's checks, not even any proof of our identity."

Tina is biting her nails. This is all too much for her. When Karl sees her looking like that he can imagine how she is feeling. Probably all she wants to do now is go home and never see him again.

Karl's bottle of wine is still half full. Hastily, he drinks what is left of it. The game's up, Karl Fechner, he tells himself. You're the victim this time.

Tina asks, in a small voice, "Who could have stolen it? There aren't any bad people here, are there?"

"How do you think bad people look?" asks Karl. "How do thieves look? How do people who kidnap children look?"

"They look like you," says Tina quietly.

They push back their chairs and leave the café, slinking back to the supermarket like beaten dogs, and Woof himself follows with his tail between his legs, as if he had understood every word they said. But he is a Spanish dog.

"I'm worn out," says Karl, beginning to undress. He is not only worn out but slightly drunk on the heavy red wine, and his head hurts; so does his heart. He lies down on his cot.

"I want to go home to Mommy." Suddenly Tina is not a big girl anymore, but very small. "Mommy, Mommy!" She throws herself on her bed, crumples up the bedclothes, and cries.

"No," says Karl. "No, they won't get me that way!"

And suddenly Tina is furious. She plants herself in

front of Karl's bed and yells, "I want to go home this minute, and if you don't take me home this minute I'll call Mommy, and I'll tell the police about you, and you'll go to jail!"

Karl sits up, stares at Tina in astonishment, and then he raises his hand and slaps her face. Tina staggers back and falls against the shelves. No one has hit her in her entire life. Karl rubs his hand and looks down at the floor. He didn't mean to hit her, really he didn't. He never wanted to hit her.

T I N A

Father. Why did you do that? Why?

My cheek is burning, I'm lying on the cold floor, and I can't even cry.

I just want to go home.

Mother would never hit me.

Father is sitting on the bed, his head hanging.

The shutter squeals when I raise it enough to go out.

"Tina!" I hear Father call after me.

No. It's too late now.

I run down the road to the sea. There's a full moon, and the road is empty.

It's creepy.

I'm alone. I'm all alone in the world.

No, I'm not. Woof comes panting after me.

Go away, Woof. I don't want to play.

I kick Woof. Oh, no, Woof, I'm sorry, I didn't mean to do that, Woof. Please forgive me.

I run and run. I can feel sand under my feet again. Woof is still behind me.

There they are, up ahead. They're still there. I run faster and faster, until I'm out of breath.

Inge stands up and puts her arms around me.

"It's all right, Tina, it's all right . . ."

I can't say a word. My chest hurts from running so fast.

Inge sits down again, cradling my head in her lap. She strokes my hair.

"Take it easy," she murmurs. "You can tell me later . . . take it easy now . . ."

My breathing is more regular again. I can feel the warmth of the fire; it's almost out now, but still smoldering. Someone is playing a guitar, there's a sweet smell in the air, and all the faces look beautiful in the light of the full moon.

The man playing the guitar begins a new song. I know it—Mother has it on a record. It's about the little tin soldier with only one leg, who gets thrown away, and then he floats into the sea and gets fished out and makes a lot more children happy, and he finds the little ballerina doll he used to love.

The full moon has moved on a bit. Woof is sniffing around the remains of the food. He gets hold of a bone and gnaws on it.

My eyes are closed. I'd like to go to sleep, but I can't. My thoughts are wide-awake inside my head and racing frantically about. They make me cry. Inge doesn't say anything, just lets me cry till I can't cry anymore.

I sit up and wipe my eyes. It's quieter now; a lot of the people are lying down to sleep behind the sand dunes, wrapped in blankets. And the babies are sleeping as peacefully as if they were in a real, soft bed.

The sea sounds louder than usual. I expect that's because of the full moon. I look up. I don't care what people say, there *is* a man in the moon. I can see his face quite clearly. Never mind if the features are really craters—maybe they are if you're on the moon, but from here they're a face. How do I know how a fly feels if it gets up my nostril? It probably thinks it's in some terrifying, creepy cave. But it's only my nostril.

Inge follows my gaze. "I live up there," she says. "That little mark beside the right eye—can you see it? That's my house."

"And there's where *I* live!" There's a dimple beside the man in the moon's mouth. A great, wide valley, where I've settled down with Tim.

"And Mother and Father live on the other side of the moon," I say. "They can come and visit Tim and me sometimes."

"Right up in the moon? I always thought your father had his head in the clouds!" says Inge. It's a joke.

"Well, he doesn't," I say, rather sulkily. I can't bear other people to say anything against Father. "He hit me," I say. "He was so horrible to me, really horrible, he's never done that before!"

Inge nods. So now she knows why I was so miserable. "And now you're angry with him, right?"

94

I nod, clenching my jaw. Yes. The anger is still there inside me. I could . . . I'd like to . . . I clench my fists, too.

"Wow, you do look dangerous!" says Inge, and quite suddenly my anger is all gone.

"Have you ever hit anyone?" I ask.

Inge nods. "Mmm," she says. "My boyfriend."

"Was he horrible to you, too?"

Inge shakes her head. "No. I had gone to pieces at the time, you see—everything had gone wrong. I'd failed an exam, I'd had a fight with my father, and I didn't have a penny to my name, and then Manfred started going on about something . . ." Inge thinks, then laughs. "You see, I can't even remember *why* I did it! But I had all this anger inside me and it had to come out somehow!"

"There's a lot of anger inside Father, too," I say. "He's afraid as well."

"Yes, I know," says Inge.

And then I tell her all about it, starting with the day Father met me outside school with his black canvas bag packed. I tell her about Tim, and Mother, and school, and how much I love them all, and how I'd like to go home to Mother but all the same I don't want Father to be so lonely, and I just want to keep all of it: Mother, Father, Tim, Cactus, and Slow-and-Solid. And I want everything to stay the way it used to be.

Inge shakes her head.

"That was bad, his taking you away like that. It could get him into all sorts of trouble. And when I think of your mother I feel sick—she must be out of her mind with worry!"

I nod sadly. I've been trying not to think about that too much, and now I can suddenly see Mother in my mind's eye, all pale and bent and red-eyed, and I swallow.

Inge scratches her nose. "Things can't be the way they used to be. Are you the way you used to be?"

"No," I say. "I'm big now! I used to be little and silly, and I was always doing stupid things, but it's different now that I'm big. I think."

"When you're big you do other stupid things," says Inge. "Karl and your mother are still growing, too. Not upwards, but inside their heads and their hearts. You think people just wake up one morning and find they're grown-up? Well, they don't. Growing up goes on all the time. Sometimes you grow a little wiser, then you grow a little prettier, or otherwise; then you get a bit more sense of humor, or you become a little more serious. . . . Maybe when you're ninety you'll be able to say: Well, Tina, now you've finished growing up and you've done a good job of it. On the other hand, when you're ninety you may be moaning and groaning and wondering if you will ever grow up!"

And Inge rolls her eyes. I can't help laughing, but all the same I shift about on the sand uneasily. I can't stand still, because of Father. Is he asleep? Is he lying awake? Is he looking for me? No. This is the first place he'd come. . . .

"I won't say much more," says Inge, "but you know, ever since Anna was born I've been thinking a lot about things like growing up and getting old." She points to the sleeping baby. "I'm her mother now. I'll be her mother all my life. But I'm also Inge, a separate human being, and Inge, a masseuse who wants to study medicine, and I'd like to be Dr. Inge, and Inge who's the girl friend of some splendid man, and Inge the farmer, and Inge the world traveler, and Inge the mountaineer. I'm a lot of things, and I'd like to be everything. So would everyone, including your father, and I bet your mother would, too. Only they don't quite dare—they keep falling over their own feet."

I imagine Mother and Father walking along side by side and falling flat on their faces the whole time. It makes me giggle.

"Well, all that talking, and I only mean it's not easy for them, either." Inge yawns and rubs her face. "Am I tired!" She yawns again, and it makes me yawn, too.

I must go back to Father. I want to go back to Father. "Woof!" I call softly. Woof gets up and shakes himself.

"We've lost our money, too," I tell Inge. How funny I only remembered that just now, and yet it was what really spoiled our Christmas Eve!

I look up at the sky again. Not a comet in sight. Oh, well, it was two thousand years ago.

"Oh, how awful," says Inge. "I'm sorry, I really am! I don't have much left myself." She thinks. "But perhaps something will occur to me. Sleep well, and dream of something nice, and tell your father to stop this nonsense."

"What nonsense?"

"Everything he's doing right now."

"I'll tell him," I say, waving good-bye. Woof and I run back to Father.

The shutter squeals again. It needs some oil.

Father doesn't hear me. He's lying on his stomach, asleep, snoring gently. I sit down on the floor beside him and look at him. He doesn't look grown-up when he's asleep. His mouth is open, and the ends of his mustache flutter when he breathes out. It would drive me crazy to have hair fluttering around my mouth like that!

"I love you, Father," I whisper, giving him a little kiss on the forehead.

I feel rather noble, but all the same I say, "You shouldn't have hit me, though." Father grunts in his sleep and turns over.

"You'll roast in hell for that," I add, and then I feel terrible. What a thing to say!

Nonsense. There's no such place as hell, anyway.

ANGELICA

Angelica and Tim have had a very sad Christmas Eve. Tim unwrapped his presents under the Christmas tree without much enthusiasm. The tree was decorated, but it didn't look very good this year. When Angelica began singing "Silent Night" in a sad voice, Tim didn't want to play with his railway set anymore. He toyed with his food and soon went to bed to listen to two new cassettes of fairy tales. Angelica went to the medicine cabinet, opened and then closed it again a couple of times, and finally decided she would take a sleeping tablet after all, although she does not approve of taking pills.

What luck Grandma didn't come for Christmas. That would have made everything even worse, when Grandma doesn't know about Karl kidnapping Tina.

On Christmas morning Angelica wakes up with a headache. Her throat hurts.

Tim is whining in the doorway. "Will breakfast be ready soon?"

Angelica sits upright in bed and stares at her son as if she were seeing him for the very first time. The walls seem to quiver. "Breakfast . . . will . . . not . . . be ready soon!" shrieks Angelica, and the next minute, face twisted with pain, she clutches at her throat and falls back on the pillows.

Tim leaves as fast as he can, sucking his thumb.

Cactus hides under the table, and Slow-and-Solid has not put in an appearance at all.

Tim opens the door of the bedroom again. "*Damn Tina!*" he bellows, and slams the door shut. He runs to his room, turns the key on the inside of the door, and turns on his cassette recorder.

Zonk.

I'm hungry. So hungry it actually woke me up. Very quietly, I get dressed. I'd like to be a dog. Woof just has to stand up and shake himself, and that's it. No need to wash or put any clothes on, and he doesn't pee until he goes outside.

No money. How are we going to pay for our breakfast today? Father's still snoring softly.

I'm not angry with him anymore. And he'll get his Christmas present from me today, a very special present: I'll get us some breakfast.

If Father's done something he shouldn't for me, then I can do something I shouldn't for him. He can't mind that. The squeal of the shutter scares me again. Even Woof jumps when he hears it. Very slowly, so as not to wake Father, I pull the shutter down again. He's fast asleep. A little ray of sunlight slips through the crack in the shutter and gropes its way toward Father.

Woof knows where I'm going. He runs ahead of me, sniffing to the right and the left and lifting his leg everywhere. He can't possibly drink enough to make all that pee!

Woof leads me down to the harbor. There are three gray boats bobbing in the water. I've come too late to watch the fish being unloaded. That's a pity. But I can smell them. Two cats are fighting over a pile of tiny, dead fish, not in the least afraid of Woof. Woof wants some of the fish, too, but he retreats with his ears back and his tail between his legs when the cats arch their backs and spit at him.

There's a lot of clanging noise coming from the bar in that white building at the corner of the harbor; the video game has everyone's attention. A fisherman with short legs is shooting down fighter planes. Father never lets me play that sort of game because it has to do with war. I think shooting and so on is silly, too, but I like playing with the video games, only I have to do it on the sly, of course.

Anyway, you can't do anything without money.

"Hey, *niña!*" calls a fisherman. He means me. He smiles at me, showing his bad teeth. I know him; we found him lying drunk on the dock once and pulled him a little way back from the water, because we were afraid he might fall in.

I smile back, rather annoyed to find him here. I hope he won't keep looking my way.

Woof lies down under the bar stools, and I climb up on one. "*Leche caliente,*" I say. That means "hot milk," and it's all the Spanish I know. No, wait, I know some more: *Gracias* means "thank you," and *cerveza* means "beer," and *adios* means "good-bye."

The woman behind the bar is wearing a knee-length skirt with sweat pants under it, a man's shirt, and a headscarf. It looks funny, but somehow I can't imagine her in anything else.

She adds hot foam from the espresso machine to a glass of milk and shifts the glass from hand to hand.

There's a plastic container on the counter with frosted buns in it. I act as if I am not at all interested in them and sip my milk. It feels good inside me, all nice and warm, and filling, too.

The woman is cleaning her espresso machine. Two more fishermen have gone over to the video game. Woof gets up and goes to the door, where he stands waiting for me. This is a good moment. Quick as lightning, I put my hand under the cover of the container, grab three frosted buns with both hands, stuff them down my pants, leave my empty milk glass where it is, jump off the stool, and dash out.

"Hey!" The woman is shouting something after me, but I don't stop, not now. Woof is panting along behind me. He can't know what's going on. Is there someone following? Before I turn the corner I see the ends of the woman's headscarf flying. Damn!

One of the buns falls down the leg of my pants, reaches my knee, and now it's in the road. I bend to pick it up and lose time. The woman is bigger than me, and she can run just as fast.

Woof thinks we're playing a game. He keeps trying to jump up at me.

I get to our supermarket, push the shutter up, and run in. I fling the buns on the bed. Father wakes up with a start, alarmed.

I am so worked up I have forgotten to pull the shutter down again. Now the woman from the bar is standing in the middle of the room, screaming, and I can't understand a word, but I know she is furious. You can catch the sound of fury in any language. She's right, too.

I slink away into a corner, trembling. Such a disgrace, getting caught! I'm scared.

Father has no idea what is happening, but then he seems to understand. He says something to the woman, and she calms down a bit. Father gives her the buns back, and she goes away. I close my eyes and put my hands over my ears and press my lips together.

Father's there in front of me: I can see him if I peer through my eyelids. I can hear, vaguely, that he's saying something, and I slowly take my hands away from my ears.

He kneels down in front of me and looks at me. I just look back. Father holds out his arms. I go into them and he holds me tight. He doesn't say anything else, not now.

We crouch there for quite a long time, and I'd like to stay there forever. Well, now we've both done something silly. First Father, then me. I'm his daughter, after all.

K A R L

Karl Fechner is just about the worst father in the world, as he realizes very clearly at that moment, holding Tina in his arms. He ought never to have gotten her into such a situation. His daughter stealing because she's hungry, and he is unable to buy her any breakfast!

Karl feels like a piece of meat that has been beaten out by the butcher. Beaten too long, no juice left in it. He's finished. He comes to a decision.

"Tina."

"Mmm?" says Tina. By now she feels so comfortable in Karl's arms that she'd like to stay there for good.

"I still have our return tickets for the ferry," he says. "We'll catch the afternoon boat and go to the German Consulate in Tenerife. They'll be able to tell Mother where we are, and then we'll fly home."

"You and me?" asks Tina. She doesn't know whether to feel glad, or scared, or what.

"Both of us." Karl nods.

"What about the police? Will they arrest you?"

Karl nods again. "I think so," he says, suddenly looking away. He tightens his lips and swallows, the way you do when you have to cry but you wish you didn't.

T I N A

I'm going down to the sea. I want to say good-bye to Inge. But as luck will have it I can't find Inge, or little Pierre, or any of Inge's friends.

I go back again, depressed, and help Father pack. I get my bathing suit out of the bag, and then take back the empty bottles to get the deposit on them. That's our bus fare.

The waves are very big today.

I have to go into the sea once more. I fling myself into the waves as if I really had to show the sea what I can do, this last time. I swim around the rocks like a fish, though they can be very dangerous, but I'm careful not to swim too close. I peer over the crest of a wave. Does this sea go all the way to South America? Has this very wave been there already? I feel odd. I'm not wildly happy to be going home. I feel as if I've lost something, too. I'm even a little bit angry with Father. Why does he give up so easily? He had such wonderful dreams.

Well, so much for his dreams. A pity. Or is it?

When I come back to the supermarket, wet and shivering, Father and Woof are waiting impatiently. Father has a towel ready for my wet bathing suit, and I squeeze into my trousers with some difficulty, because I'm still wet.

"What about Woof?" I ask, patting him.

"Woof will have to stay here," says Father, stroking him, too. "He'll find other friends."

"Oh, Woof!" I kneel down and put my arms around his neck.

Woof looks unmoved. Or perhaps he understands everything after all, because when we go away he just stays there, tail at half-mast, watching us as we disappear around the corner.

He doesn't follow.

I feel a large, sad hole inside me, where Woof was, and I try to fill it up by thinking of Cactus. We go slowly along the beach and then up the road to the bus stop. It's hot, and we sit down to wait on the white wall that runs between the street and the banana plantation. Several people come past and say hello, as usual, raising a hand. Father has had enough of that kind of thing. "Easy come, easy go," he mutters.

Pierre happens to come by. That's nice. He sits down beside me chewing a banana leaf, says something, which Father translates as, "See you next year!" and then goes on a little sadly. "Well, there's at least one person sorry to see us go," says Father.

"Maybe!" I shout after Pierre, but by now he can't hear me anymore.

K A R L

A car comes downhill along the road, brakes squealing. The Valle Gran Rey police car.

Karl sits there perfectly still, hands clutching at the little wall.

The car comes to a sudden halt in front of Tina and her father. Karl pushes himself away from the wall and stands up. His arms are hanging limp at his sides, and Tina can see that he's trembling. A policeman gets out.

And Tina starts moving; she jumps between Karl and the policeman, shouting, "Don't you dare arrest him! Keep your hands off my father!"

The back door of the car opens, and Inge gets out. Tina and Karl are totally at a loss. Tina glares angrily at Inge. So she told the police all about the kidnapping!

The policeman smiles at Tina rather awkwardly and raises his eyebrows.

Karl tells himself he will not say a word—not now—

he'll wait until he can tell his story to the German police.

"Karl-Heinz Fechner?" asks the policeman, pronouncing his name with a heavy Spanish accent, but there is no doubt that that is what he is saying.

"Listen..." says Inge, but Karl turns away, and the policeman won't give Inge a chance to speak.

He puts something into Karl's hand. Karl, confused, takes it; then the policeman salutes Tina, Inge, and Karl, says, "*Adios!*" and gets into his car and drives away, tires squealing, flinging up dust and dead banana leaves behind him.

"They have a television set in the local police station—they spend all day watching American thrillers," says Inge.

Karl is holding his wallet. He can hardly believe it. Feverishly, he looks through it: Everything is there. His passport, traveler's checks, papers, cash, address book.

"The money!" cries Tina happily.

"An American found it under a bush outside the El Cid and handed it in this morning," says Inge. "Nobody knew where you were staying. I didn't know myself, and since I've known the policeman for some time we've been driving around looking for you."

Karl puts his arms around Inge.

"I just don't know how to thank you," he says, but Inge waves his thanks away.

"Well, you can invite me for a meal now!" she says. Baby Anna, slung in front of Inge as usual, smiles and sucks her tiny thumb. Karl takes Tina right across the street to the El Cid café. They fall into the place like starving cats on a trash can. Inge does not eat much, just the apple dumpling that Tina recommends. That nice woman from the previous evening is eating in the café. Beaming, Karl pays her back, and thanks her yet again.

"Could happen to anyone!" she says, smiling at Tina. "You're hungry, aren't you?" she says to her.

Tina nods. As her plate empties she chews more slowly. "Father?" she asks.

Karl knows what Tina wants to ask.

"We're still catching that ferry, Tina," he says. And Tina shovels in her delicious goulash as fast as ever.

Inge smiles. "I hope my daughter won't be quite so greedy, or I'll have trouble feeding her!"

Tina gets up and gives Inge a goulash-flavored kiss on her cheek, although it is not at all the polite thing to do.

"I just wanted to tell you I think you're terrific," she says, ordering herself another big bottle of orange soda.

ANGELICA

"You've been working too hard, Mrs. Fechner," says the man in the white coat, bending over his prescription pad. "Just take these pills; they'll calm you down and help you to sleep better."

"I don't need any pills," says Angelica. "I only wanted

to know if I'm all right." She puts her skirt back on; it has gotten too big for her over the last few days.

"Well, I can't make you take anything!" says the doctor, crumpling up the prescription form. "I daresay you know best."

"Yes," says Angelica, nodding. "Good-bye."

She shivers in the cold air outside and trudges home on foot. Snow fell last night, and the city looks attractive; it is still cold enough for the snow to stick.

Angelica looks around. Her footprints are almost the only ones on the pavement.

"Damn him," she mutters, "damn him, damn him, damn him." Every time she says *damn* she stamps on the snow harder, so that her tracks look as if they had been made by someone with feet of different sizes.

She will never be able to forgive Karl for what he's done to her. When is he going to get in touch? And how exactly does he feel about what he has done? He probably doesn't see it at all. Karl never thought very much about anything. Angelica remembers all the ideas he used to get and put into practice, just like that, whereupon he very often fell flat on his face. Although sometimes he did succeed in the most surprising ways.

"Huh!" says Angelica bitterly, out loud. A man passing her in the opposite direction looks at her, startled. "Peculiar young woman, talking to herself," he mutters, and realizing that he is talking to himself, too, he shuts his mouth and walks on, faster.

Angelica pursues her own thoughts.

Perhaps Karl is somewhere in the South Seas now, amusing himself with beautiful young girls while a nanny looks after Tina. Where would he get the money for that sort of thing? Or he's sailing around the world with Tina on a yacht—that was always one of his daydreams. Or ...

"I want to do what *I* want, too!" cries Angelica, kicking up snow. She has reached home. There's a light on in the playroom, and she can hear Cactus snuffling on the other side of the door.

Angelica feels a pang: She'll never get used to living with just Tim, as much as she loves him. She has two children, Tim *and* Tina. Only where is Tina now?

T I N A

Father's much more cheerful going back on the boat than he was coming. In fact, he's in a *wonderful* mood, walking all around the ferry and telling me about everything. I think he's glad it'll soon be over. He isn't even scared of jail anymore.

I don't want them to send Father to jail. He's not a criminal; he hasn't hurt anyone. Except for slapping me, but I don't think they put your parents in jail for that, unless they hit you really hard and somebody complains to the police.

We come in to land. It's dark by the time we leave the ferry, and Father and I go into the first hotel we see.

"I think we've picked the most expensive one," he

whispers to me at the reception desk. "Is there a telephone in the room?" he asks the man in the hat, who seems to own all the keys on the big board.

Yes, there's a telephone in our room: a big black one, standing between the two beds. Father sits down and looks at it, closes his eyes, opens them again, and puts his hand out to pick up the receiver.

I hold my breath as he dials the number. He is biting his lower lip. There is no sound from the receiver for quite a long time, and then faint clicking noises. Father clears his throat.

"It's me," he says. Then nothing happens. Father keeps quiet, holding the receiver close to his ear and closing his eyes. I go around the bed and sit behind Father. I can hear it now, too. The sound of crying. Mother is crying.

"We're coming home," says Father, and then he puts the receiver into my hand.

"Mother?" It's quite odd to hear Mother's voice: It sounds so small and far away. I feel warm all over with happiness, and I get pins and needles in my legs, perhaps because I'd like to magically transport myself along the telephone lines and into Mother's arms. Over the sea and the mountains and the valleys.

Mother doesn't know what to say. "I just don't know what to say, darling," she sobs, and then she laughs, and then she cries again.

Sitting on the bed beside me, Father is so worked up he blows his nose on the bedspread.

"Mother wants to know when we'll be arriving."

"Tell her we'll be on the first plane tomorrow!"

111

"We'll be on the first plane tomorrow!" I say, and Mother says she'll meet me—she doesn't say anything about Father. Then there's a crackling, grumbling sound, and Mother says there must be an elephant on the line, and then, suddenly, she's gone.

I put down the receiver, and Father picks it up, but there really isn't any more to hear.

We cuddle and then we go to sleep. It's strange that I can sleep so well when I'm so excited.

K A R L

"But we *must* have seats!" Karl is standing at the air-line desk, shifting nervously from foot to foot.

"Mr. Fechner, as I've already told you, if two seats happen to be free you will be welcome to them, but I'm afraid you will have to wait for another twenty minutes. The plane is fully booked!"

"Yes, I know," says Karl, taking a bill out of his recently recovered wallet and showing it to the girl at the desk.

"I can't promise you any more, however much money there is in it!" she snaps.

Disappointed, Karl puts the money away again.

Tina is feeling impatient. "Now what do we do, Father?"

Karl shrugs his shoulders. "We wait, Tina." He does

not move from the spot. They watch passenger after passenger producing tickets. Then they all go through. The girl at the desk looks at a list, and then smiles. "You're in luck, Mr. Fechner. There are two seats free!"

"Hurray!" shouts Tina, skipping around in a circle. She hadn't realized before how scared she was they might not get on the plane. Mother would have been standing at the airport, looking and looking, and Karl and Tina would not have gotten off that airplane.

But it is all right now. Relieved, Karl picks up the black canvas bag and takes Tina's hand.

"Have a good flight!"

"Thanks." Karl smiles and goes through customs and the passport check with Tina.

"We ought to have brought Woof along after all," says Tina, going up the steps of the plane.

The engines are running, and then they are high up in the blue sky. Down below are the mountains in the sea. "Gomera!" cries Tina, pressing her nose to the window. Inge is down there somewhere, with Anna slung around her, or maybe she's feeding Anna at this moment.

Perhaps Woof is sniffing around the supermarket, still following the scent of Karl and Tina. Perhaps he thinks they'll be coming back. Or perhaps he is looking up at the sky right now, and knows Tina is in the big bird up there. . . .

"Feeling a little sad?" asks Karl, putting his arm around her shoulders. Tina nods, squeezes out a tear for Woof, one for Inge and Anna, one for the blue sea, and then begins to look forward to seeing Mother and Tim.

Karl is very quiet during the five hours of the flight. Tina can understand that; she senses that he is all strung up, as if he were facing an exam. And he must be scared, too.

A N G E L I C A

Tim does not want to go with her. "I couldn't stand it," he says. "I'd rather listen to 'Snow White and Rose Red.' "

Angelica looks disappointed at first, but then she is glad she can go to the airport by herself. Just for once she takes two spoonfuls of valerian drops to calm her down.

She calls a taxi, and when she reaches the airport she is an hour and a half early, so she has five cups of coffee, which cancel out the calming effects of the valerian drops.

Angelica's heart is beating wildly. It scares her. She watches planes take off and land, follows their flight as far as the eye can see, and tries to sit still. She misses hearing the announcement that the plane from Tenerife has landed on time. Then she runs to Gate 8 at the last minute. Is it always so hot in this place?

"Mother!" I'm running, racing, stumbling, and then I'm holding her tight. I take a deep breath. Mother smells the same as ever.

"I feel sick," says Mother, but she doesn't let go of my hand; she drags me off to the ladies' room with her.

"Wait a minute!" Mother disappears behind a red door, and I can hear her throwing up. Throwing up all the anxiety of the last couple of weeks into a white toilet. She flushes it and comes out again.

She is red in the face, but beaming.

"I'm better now—oh, Tina, darling!" We go out of the ladies' room together, and there is Father, clutching the black canvas bag and looking at the floor.

Mother squeezes my hand.

She goes up to Father, and there is a sharp sound. Father drops the black canvas bag and puts a hand to his cheek—and then she slaps the other cheek. Both his cheeks are red.

I can't help laughing. Mother is jumping up and down in front of Father, scolding him and raging at him, just like Rumpelstiltskin, and people stop to watch—not that Mother notices.

Father doesn't know just what to do, but he takes a step toward Mother and puts his arms around her, and they both start crying.

I stand around feeling a bit silly with all this going on. I wouldn't have believed parents could behave this way, least of all *my* parents. Through Father's sobs I can hear something about "the police," and through

Mother's sobs I can make out that she's saying, "No, of course not!" And then Father gives Mother a kiss on the cheek.

"Don't do that, Karl," says Mother, crying, and she goes on crying while Father searches for handkerchiefs. Mother tries to take Father's black canvas bag and carry it to the taxi stand. Everything is very strange. I feel like shouting, "Listen, I'm still here, you know!"

Oh, well. I trot off after them. What's up now? Do they love each other again, or what? Anyway, I'm looking forward to seeing Tim, and Slow-and-Solid, and Cactus.

You bet I am.

AFTERWORD

Since this book has a foreword it ought to have an afterword, too.

It cannot be said that Angelica, Karl, Tina, and Tim Fechner are going to live happily ever after. At first Father visits the family every day, has meals with the children, plays with them, takes an interest in what they are doing at school just as he used to, goes on trips with them, and does not argue with Angelica. Angelica does not argue with him, either. It almost looks as if they could forgive each other for the past and are beginning to love one another again.

This happy state of affairs lasts four weeks. Then comes the first argument.

But now they are on their guard, and the first argument is the only one. The Fechners decide to think of a solution that will work for all of them. Karl turns one room of his apartment into a room for Tim and Tina. Tim has made up with his father, and the children go live with both their parents. Sometimes one of them wants to stay with Father, sometimes both of them, sometimes they would rather be with Mother. And this actually does work, probably because Father's apartment is not very far away. However, it is no use for them all to try living together again, the way they used to. Karl and Angelica have grown too far apart for that. It certainly hurts Karl when he learns that Angelica has a boyfriend who stays overnight, and the children like him. But you just have to get used to such things, and no doubt Karl will not spend the rest of his life without another woman, either.

So for the time being, all is more or less peaceful. Tim and Tina feel quite happy. Slow-and-Solid has not learned to talk yet, and Cactus still gets under the bed when no one is looking and leaves his hairs about for people to sweep up.

What will happen next? No one knows.

Things can always change.